Bottom-Tier Character TOMOZAKI

Lv.8.5

YUKI YAKU

Illustration by

Fly

Three sisters

"So then... we're both drunk?"

Chocolate Disco

Bottom-Tier
Character Tomozaki, Level 8.5

CONTENTS

Fuka Kikuchi

Design Yuko Mucadeya + Caiko Monma
(musicagographics)

Bottom-Tier Character Tomozaki

Lv.8.5

Yuki Yaku

Illustration by Fly

Yen On
New York

Bottom-Tier CHARACTER TOMOZAKI Lv.8.5

YUKI YAKU

Cover art by Fly
Translation by Winifred Bird

JAKU CHARA TOMOZAKI-KUN LV.8.5
by Yuki YAKU
© 2016 Yuki YAKU
Illustration by FLY
All rights reserved.
Original Japanese edition published by SHOGAKUKAN.
English translation rights in the United States of America, Canada, the United Kingdom, Ireland, Australia, and New Zealand arranged with SHOGAKUKAN through Tuttle-Mori Agency, Inc.

English translation © 2022 by Yen Press, LLC

Yen On
150 West 30th Street, 19th Floor
New York, NY 10001

Visit us at yenpress.com
facebook.com/yenpress
twitter.com/yenpress
yenpress.tumblr.com
instagram.com/yenpress

First Yen On Edition: September 2022
Edited by Yen On Editorial: Anna Powers
Designed by Yen Press Design: Wendy Chan

Yen On is an imprint of Yen Press, LLC.
The Yen On name and logo are trademarks of Yen Press, LLC.

Library of Congress Cataloging-in-Publication Data
Names: Yaku, Yuki, author. | Fly, 1963- illustrator. | Bird, Winifred, translator.
Title: Bottom-tier character Tomozaki / Yuki Yaku ; illustration by Fly ; translation by Winifred Bird.
Other titles: Jyakukyara Tomozaki-kun. English
Description: First Yen On edition. | New York : Yen On, 2019-
Identifiers: LCCN 2019017466 | ISBN 9781975358259 (v. 1 : pbk.) | ISBN 9781975384586 (v. 2 : pbk.) |
   ISBN 9781975384593 (v. 3 : pbk.) | ISBN 9781975384609 (v. 4 : pbk.) | ISBN 9781975384616 (v. 5 : pbk.) |
   ISBN 9781975384623 (v. 6 : pbk.) | ISBN 9781975320386 (v. 6.5 : pbk.) | ISBN 9781975333461 (v. 7 : pbk.) |
   ISBN 9781975335502 (v. 8 : pbk.) | ISBN 9781975338404 (v. 8.5 : pbk.)
Subjects: LCSH: Video games—Fiction. | Video gamers—Fiction.
Classification: LCC PL877.5.A35 J9313 2019 | DDC 895.63/6—dc23
LC record available at https://lccn.loc.gov/2019017466

ISBNs: 978-1-9753-3840-4 (paperback)
       978-1-9753-3925-8 (ebook)

10 9 8 7 6 5 4 3 2 1

LSC-C

Printed in the United States of America

Bottom-Tier CHARACTER TOMOZAKI

Lv.8.5

Characters

Fumiya Tomozaki
Second-year high school student. Bottom-tier.

Aoi Hinami
Second-year high school student. Perfect heroine of the school.

Minami Nanami
Second-year high school student. Class clown.

Hanabi Natsubayashi
Second-year high school student. Small.

Yuzu Izumi
Second-year high school student. Hot.

Fuka Kikuchi
Second-year high school student. Bookworm.

Takahiro Mizusawa
Second-year high school student. Wants to be a beautician.

Shuji Nakamura
Second-year high school student. Class boss.

Takei
Second-year high school student. Built.

Tsugumi Narita
First-year high school student. Easygoing.

Erika Konno
Second-year high school student. Queen of the class.

Rena
Twenty years old. Likes to drink.

Common Honorifics

In order to preserve the authenticity of the Japanese setting of this book, we have chosen to retain the honorifics used in the original language to express the relationships between characters.

No honorific: Indicates familiarity or closeness; if used without permission or reason, addressing someone in this manner would constitute an insult.

-*san*: The Japanese equivalent of Mr./Mrs./Miss. If a situation calls for politeness, this is the fail-safe honorific.

-*kun*: Used most often when referring to boys, this indicates affection or familiarity. Occasionally used by older men among their peers, but it may also be used by anyone referring to a person of lower standing.

-*chan*: An affectionate honorific indicating familiarity used mostly in reference to girls; also used in reference to cute persons or animals of either gender.

-*senpai*: An honorific indicating respect for a senior member of an organization. Often used by younger students with their upperclassmen at school.

-*sensei*: An honorific indicating respect for a master of some field of study. Perhaps most commonly known as the form of address for teachers in school.

1

First
Christmas

Bottom-Tier Character TOMOZAKI

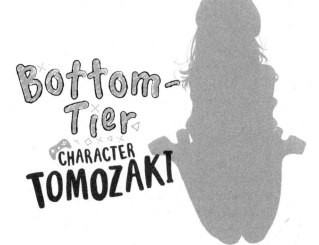

It was the day after the Sekitomo High School festival, and just over twenty kids from our class were gathered at an *okonomiyaki* restaurant in Omiya.

"Ahem! Good evening, everybody! Thank you for joining me here today!"

Izumi was standing in front of the group, giving a speech.

"Um, so the manga café and play organized by second-year Class Two were both a stunning success. I feel very gratified by the outcome…"

"Yuzu! Relax a little!" Kashiwazaki-san teased.

"Oh, um, okay?! Uh…"

Izumi was so nervous, she was talking like the principal or something. She glanced around anxiously, stared at her left palm for a second, nodded vigorously, then started talking again. Something was definitely written on her hand.

"T-today we are celebrating with a combined school festival party and Christmas party. Please enjoy yourselves…um…"

"Seriously, chill out!"

"Uh, um…"

After practicing her speech and/or writing it on her hand, her friend's heckling had thrown her off course.

"It's cold out there, so please…um…"

"You can do this!"

"…Oh, I give up!!"

Apparently out of desperation, she raised the glass she was holding over her head.

"Uh, cheers!!"

"Cheers!" everyone responded, clinking their glasses of soda in response to her rambling toast.

It was December 24—Christmas Eve—and I was there with everyone else to celebrate our school festival success. The toast kicked off an outburst of excited chatter as the party got going. We were seated around a long table set with six hot plates for cooking the *okonomiyaki* pancakes, with friends sitting together.

"Yeah! This is gonna be wild!"

Unfortunately, Takei was sitting to my right, and he seemed to be shouting directly into my ear. I scowled, but this only caused him to wrap his arm jovially around my shoulder.

"So, Farm Boy, you're gonna let loose tonight, right?"

"Shut up, Takei."

"You're so mean!"

Since I don't feel nervous around Takei anymore, I'm very honest with him. I *might* have been a little rude just then—no, on second thought, that approach was probably perfect for Takei.

Mizusawa and Nakamura were sitting across from us, with Tachibana, Kyoya Hashiguchi, and other jocks on either side of them. Daichi Matsumoto, who also belongs to that group, was to my left. Scanning my surroundings, I realized I was the only one with an obviously lower strength in the game of life, but I could crush them at *Atafami*, at least. Call it a draw?

"Ah-ha-ha, you're so harsh to Takei, Tomozaki," Matsumoto said.

"Uh, oh, I am?" I sputtered, thrown off slightly by his directness.

I wasn't mentally prepared for it, but apparently the jock group was starting to feel that I belonged here simply because I hung out with Nakamura's group. I wish they'd stop. I'm not ready for the friend-of-a-friend-is-a-friend thing yet.

The kids gathered around the long table were roughly divided by gender, and the border between girls and guys was nearby. That was probably because of Nakamura's stronghold. Hinami's group—which included her, Mimimi, Kashiwazaki-san, and Seno-san—was right by Takei. At the moment, Izumi was there, too, stopping by in her role as president of the festival organizing committee.

"Nice job with the festival, Yuzucchi!"

"Thanks, Takei!"

"You're gonna raise the roof with us, right, Yuzucchi?"

"Oh, um, of course?!"

Undaunted, Takei had turned to Izumi on his right and was chatting her up enthusiastically. Being a nice person, she answered politely. High-caliber material right there.

"Nice! I'm gonna drink myself under the table tonight! Refill!" Takei shouted, apparently drunk on cola.

"Uh, you know these are soft drinks, right?" Izumi joked.

"Chug it, Takei!" Nakamura jumped in.

"You know I will!!" he shot back.

Hinami and Izumi smiled and clapped, although they looked slightly uncomfortable. I mean, why was he going to chug a soda? The only thing he'll get is a minor sugar rush. Man, I can already see these guys going overboard when they get to university.

"Hanging back, eh, Director?"

I looked up at the sudden voice and saw Mizusawa smiling directly at me from across the table. Shady as always. I smiled back and shook my head.

"Uh, yeah…I can't keep up with that kind of thing," I said.

"Ha-ha-ha. Not surprised." Mizusawa seemed impressed by Takei and the others. "I'm not so into it myself."

"You're not? Really?"

"Really. You don't think I'm that type, do you?"

"No…I guess not."

Even though he belongs to Nakamura's group, he tends to keep his cool in situations like this. I've never really seen him messing around like a kid, which is probably a good thing, because I can't even imagine how far off the rails those other two would go without him around.

"But seriously, Fumiya."

"What?"

"That play was really good."

"Yeah? Thanks."

Suddenly, Mizusawa was getting all sincere on me, and his expression was as cool as if he was talking about someone neither of us knew. The play that Kikuchi-san wrote for the school festival had been a smash hit—even subtracting my personal bias. I was still feeling the aftereffects two days later.

"…But aren't you kind of complimenting yourself? You had a starring role!" I joked.

Mizusawa raised his eyebrows. "Technically, but I was just a character doing what the script told me to do."

"A character… Yeah."

I can't help getting my guard up whenever I hear Mizusawa say that word. Ever since the summer barbecue, the idea of a player's perspective versus a character's perspective has been haunting our conversations.

"Oh, I don't mean in that sense. You were the one fighting the battle this time, after all."

"…Yeah…guess I was," I agreed haltingly.

When Kikuchi-san had started floundering in her attempts to be more like her "ideal," I went to Mizusawa for advice, and he really helped me figure out a way to be useful. After all that, there was no reason to mince words now. Without Mizusawa's perspective as a person who was trying to change from a player to a character, I'm fairly sure I wouldn't have picked up on the emotions beneath Kikuchi-san's ideal. And that was exactly why I felt I had to say one more thing on the subject.

"Kikuchi-san was in the battle, too," I declared.

"Definitely," he said, smiling in admiration. Relaxed as always, he glanced at her. Everyone had been invited to the party, but it must have taken a lot of courage for her to show up. She was sitting on the girls' side of the table, talking in a low voice with the girl next to her.

"She's really changed," Mizusawa said.

"…Yeah."

I scratched behind my ear shyly as if Mizusawa had just complimented me instead of her.

"I'm happy for you guys."

"How so?" I asked.

"When I read the final version of the script, I wasn't sure what would happen…but since you're dating now, I guess everything worked out," he said, cool as a cucumber.

I flinched slightly. Apparently, he'd caught on to the underlying meaning of the script.

For me and Kikuchi-san, "On the Wings of the Unknown" was a special play, because it was about the way we looked at the world.

"Uh, just how much did you figure out…?"

"Who knows? Maybe I'm just trying to trick you into spilling the beans."

"Hey now…"

As usual, his aloof attitude had me tripping over my own feet, but I wanted to hear his opinion. So far, no one had told me what they thought about the play, or the characters, or the ending. Specifically, I was curious to know what they had read between the lines.

"But you noticed some stuff in the script?"

"Of course I did. I'm a smart guy."

"Yeah, yeah."

I brushed off his egotistical act, but I wanted to know more. He might joke around when I try to tell him serious stuff, but he would never hit me where it really hurt.

"What did you think when you read it?"

He paused for a second, still smiling. "Well, actually…I thought it was pretty cruel of you to make me play that role."

"Wait, 'cruel'?"

The word caught me off guard.

"I mean, I was playing Libra, and Libra ended up with Aoi, right?" He raised one eyebrow. "Libra was supposed to be you, I assume?"

"…So you did catch that."

I couldn't deny his guess. Mimimi had noticed, too. "On the Wings of the Unknown" was about Kikuchi-san herself…and Libra was me.

Mizusawa snickered, then sighed. "You know the truth… I mean, you overheard me, right? When I was talking to Aoi on our trip."

"…S-sorry about that."

"You don't have to apologize," he said, glancing at Hinami before look-ing back at me. "But knowing that, you had me and Aoi act out a story where you and Aoi get together."

"Uh..."

"Woe is Takahiro." He laughed.

"I said I'm sorry..."

"Ha-ha-ha! It doesn't really bother me," he said casually. "In a sense, I'm jealous of you. Even if it was a play...people don't normally get that deep into personal stuff." There was a hint of emptiness in his eyes. "You were both as serious as two people can be, right?"

Still, beneath the emptiness, I glimpsed the fire of pursuit. Maybe that's why I answered so honestly.

"It was only when I faced the situation head-on that I figured out what dating her meant to me."

"...Huh."

This time, he listened without any snarky comebacks and gave me a good, long stare. Finally, his face softened.

"Anyway, I'm glad things turned out well. When I thought about that story ending the way it did...with the two of them not together... Well, I didn't know what would happen with you and her."

"S-sorry to make you worry."

"All's well that ends well. Good work, Fumiya. You can thank me for everything."

"Hey, why'd you say that?" I wasn't going to let him get away with that smooth little boast. I think I've gotten pretty good at that sort of come-back by practicing comedy sketches with Mimimi.

"Why? Well, you already admitted to copying my way of talking, and I believe I did give you quite a bit of advice."

"Okay, fine, you did..."

Mizusawa chuckled, like my awkwardness amused him. The way it annoyed me reminded me of Hinami.

"'Everything' might be an overstatement, but I'll take credit for at least a third."

"No fair, how am I supposed to argue with a third?" I shot back. But the more I thought about it, the more I felt he actually *had* saved my butt about a third of the time. *Damn, does this mean I'm in debt to him?*

"Seriously, though, I'm really happy for you."

"…Thanks."

He looked away before continuing. "Try to stay together for a while, okay? For me."

"Huh? What does that me—?" I started to ask, only to be abruptly interrupted.

"What, what?! What are you and Farm Boy talking about, Takahiro?" I'd thought Takei was occupied with the girls, but apparently not. Mizusawa turned toward him, and it was like he'd flipped a switch and turned into a completely different person.

"Oh, I was just saying how amazing the play was."

"Oh yeah!! I wanted to mention that! It was so good…"

Thanks to Takei's intrusion, the intimate atmosphere of a moment earlier evaporated instantly. That was too bad, because I was curious what Mizusawa meant by "*for me.*" But now that Takei had broken the ice, Hinami, Izumi, and Mimimi were glancing over at us and getting ready to join our conversation, so there was no way I could ask him about it now. *Guess it doesn't matter?*

"I wanted to talk about the play, too! The story was so awesome!" Izumi said innocently.

"I was great, wasn't I?" Hinami boasted.

"You were actually kinda scary!" Mimimi replied with a grin. I'm pretty sure Hinami and Mimimi both knew what the play was really about, but neither of them would bring it up in a big group like this.

"If we're going to talk about the play, we should include Kikuchi-san. Kikuchi-san!" Izumi called.

"Huh? Oh, coming…!"

She joined us, and everyone started to talk about the play.

* * *

"I couldn't attend all the rehearsals because of my other meetings, so you know when the backdrop switched to full color? I was like, oh my god!" Izumi gushed.

"Oh yeah, that was Kikuchi-san's idea. We really busted our butts to make it happen!" Hinami explained.

"I almost cried!" Kashiwazaki-san said, piling on excitedly. "You thought of that, Kikuchi-san?"

"Um, yes, I did…"

"That's amazing! I don't really know what's what with this stuff, but I think you could be a pro!"

"Wow…thank you so much…"

Kikuchi-san's voice trailed off in the face of this direct compliment from someone of her status. When Seno-san followed up with some of her own favorite parts, Kikuchi-san's face grew even redder.

As I watched, I really was happy for her. Hinami and Mizusawa and Mimimi and I were so affected by the play partly because we guessed its true meaning. But Kashiwazaki-san and Seno-san just enjoyed the story Kikuchi-san had woven, without reading anything else into it. Kikuchi-san's words, her world, had reached people who knew practically nothing about her.

"Mizusawa, you were incredible, too!"

"Ha-ha-ha. Turns out I can act, eh?"

"Ah-ha-ha! You're so annoying."

The conversation had shifted from the script to the acting. Seno-san seemed like she was having fun talking to Mizusawa. *Her eyes don't glitter like that when she talks to me. Behold, the player of a character.*

"But weren't you surprised?" Hinami asked, steering the conversation back to its original course.

Seno-san tilted her head curiously. "Surprised by what?"

"The ending—the part with the letter," Hinami said nonchalantly, but I noticed both Mizusawa and Mimimi do a double take. I'm sure my own reaction was even more obvious.

"You mean…what happened with Alucia and Libra?" Mimimi asked.

"Yeah," Hinami answered, nodding sincerely. She didn't seem to be insinuating anything, but it struck me as unnatural. For those of us who knew what the play really meant, the topic was loaded. I mean, that scene was essentially Kikuchi-san's way of rejecting me—and saying she thought Hinami and I should end up together. *That* scene.

"Oh, that...," Mizusawa said with a puzzled expression, playing it safe. Mimimi glanced back and forth between Hinami and me, then attempted to smile. She was probably trying to decide which direction to take the conversation in.

Meanwhile, Hinami was staring at Kikuchi-san with a smile. Why had she focused attention on that scene so suddenly? She probably knew that Mizusawa and Mimimi knew what it meant, not to mention the fact that Kikuchi-san and I were both here. The message in that scene would have to be especially weighty for Hinami.

"Oh, I was totally surprised! I liked Kris, so I wanted her to end up with Libra."

"You did? But it would have been so sad if Alucia ended up all alone, so I think it was better that way!"

Kashiwazaki-san and Seno-san were debating the question passionately. Their innocent opinions lightened the mood and helped me breathe a little bit easier again.

"That was...difficult to work out, for sure," Kikuchi-san said, clearly embarrassed by their comments. She glanced quickly at me. Given that the models for her characters were sitting right in front of her, I could see how she'd be struggling right now. "But I decided that within the story, that was how things should go...so I wrote it like that."

"Within the story?" Hinami interjected. I wasn't sure if she meant anything more or if the perfect heroine was just keeping the conversation going.

"I've gotta admit...I was convinced," Mizusawa said, looking straight at Hinami.

"Wait, convinced of what?" Hinami asked, meeting his gaze head-on.

"That it was the right outcome."

* * *

I understood what he was saying, but that was exactly why I didn't know how to respond. I mean, if he was saying it was right that Libra and Alucia ended up together, that meant—

Mimimi's eyes darted to Kikuchi-san in confusion, and Kikuchi-san gave me an uncomfortable glance. It was Hinami who broke the silence.

"Really? I'm not so sure."

"And why is that?" Mizusawa asked.

"After all, Alucia wanted to become a powerful queen," she answered confidently. Of course, because it was Hinami, the edges of her words were soft, and nothing she said would make those listening feel awkward. "I thought Alucia would be the most powerful queen in the world, always knowing the right thing to do, but with that ending, I'm not so sure."

Why not?

"Alucia ended up with Libra, but I think she'll be weaker that way."

It sounded to me like she was flat out rejecting the character of Alucia that Kikuchi-san had created.

"...I can see what you're saying!" Kashiwazaki-san agreed.

Hinami smiled at her. "Right?" she answered amiably. "But I'm not sure putting Libra together with Kris would have been any better. Writing plays is hard!"

"Wow, I'm starting to imagine all sorts of stuff!"

Hinami and Kashiwazaki-san continued with their fluffy conversation. I'd missed my chance, and the heart of the matter slipped away again before we could breach the surface.

"And you know the scene where they fly on the dragon..."

After that, the conversation veered toward more simplistic impressions, leaving behind the story's ending and true meaning. But this wasn't the right situation to protest.

Still, I couldn't help dwelling on it, even as the conversation flowed on and I made the requisite comments.

Mizusawa's question, Hinami's answer, and her rejection of Alucia.

If that story and its themes didn't sit right with Hinami, then what on earth *was* her ideal?

* * *

Twenty or thirty minutes passed, and the party was winding down.

"I'm glad you came today," I said to Kikuchi-san, who was taking a breather in her original seat. Everyone had been switching places and talking with various groups.

"Tomozaki-kun?"

She turned toward me, her expression relaxing. That was enough to make me happy. I grinned.

"Are you tired?" I asked.

"Um...," she said, her eyes sparkling excitedly as she searched for words. Finally, she nodded. "I'm tired, but..."

"Yeah?"

"I'm also really happy," she said with a wide, genuine smile.

"Happy...? Oh, about that." I knew exactly what she meant. "Everyone really loved the play, huh?"

"...Uh-huh." Her face flushed as she savored the moment. "The play was all about things I like...so it feels like they accepted me, too. My stomach is full of butterflies."

"Really?" I asked, smiling again.

"I'm not very good at chatting and making friends...but I'm realizing now that this is another way to interact with people."

"...Yeah, that makes sense," I answered.

I totally agreed. In the game of life, just living an ordinary life is tough. Kikuchi-san isn't naturally good at playing by its rules, but she'd found a way to do it that she was good at. It was a beautiful thing.

"And...I feel like maybe I can become friends with the people in class who enjoy the same things as me. One step at a time."

"Ha-ha. You do, huh?" I paused and thought about that for a moment. "Well, remember, you don't have to force yourself."

"What do you mean?"

I was taking care not to reject her idea. "I think I said this when we were talking about the script...but not everyone has to change to fit in with their surroundings. There's no rule saying you have to make lots of friends."

"…Okay. Thank you," she said, smiling kindly.

"But if you want to do that, then I think it's great."

"I'll think about it."

"You can always talk to me if something's bothering you."

The emotion on her face then was happy and determined at the same time. After a second, she looked up at me again.

"I know. I will," she said sincerely. That earnestness made me so happy I couldn't help smiling again.

"Oh, I almost forgot," she said, raising her voice and looking at me shyly. Her eyes sparkled with excitement.

"Tomozaki-kun… Merry Christmas."

"Oh right," I said, suddenly remembering that it was December 24. We'd only started dating two days earlier, but this was nevertheless our first Christmas as a couple.

"Yeah… Merry Christmas."

"…Thank you."

Then it dawned on me. "Sorry, I didn't get you a present or anything…"

From reading comics and stuff, I knew you were supposed to give your girlfriend a present on Christmas Eve, but Kikuchi-san just shook her head.

"Oh, that's fine… We only started two days ago…"

I'm pretty sure she meant *started dating*, but she was too shy to actually say the word. When I realized that, her shyness spread to me, and I got this kind of restless, giggly feeling.

"Um…"

"Y-yes?"

We both knew what was going on, but it was somehow hard to say directly. I guess neither of us know the right thing to do.

…In which case…

Isn't it the guy's job to take action? It was in the comics, of course. I looked her in the eye and said, "Um…but we *are* dating now. And we have plenty of time…"

I was struggling not to look away.

She nodded, blushing. "Y-yes, that's true…so…"

"Yeah?"

Then she took the plunge.

"…S-so next year, let's exchange presents."

"Huh?"

That meant we'd still be dating a year from now—my heart thumped and my brain got scrambled. *Wait a second—I thought I was good at communicating now! But Kikuchi-san always cheats.*

"Oh, uh, okay."

I looked away. Then I got worried she might think I was lying, so I turned my attention back to her. She was pouting slightly and glaring at me.

"…ise."

"What?"

She stuck out her pinkie, blushing. "Promise."

I looked at those glistening eyes peering up at me from behind her bangs and at the pinkie extended toward me. This wasn't the magic of an angel—it was a ritual offered by an amazing real-life girl.

"Oh…okay. Promise."

I hooked my own pinkie onto hers, and we sealed our pact like two little kids. What the heck? We've already held hands a couple of times, so why did our fingers feel so unbearably hot?

"—!"

We timidly pulled our hands back, both blushing.

"Your face is red, Kikuchi-san."

"Yours is, too!"

We stared at each other, then broke out laughing.

* * *

Before I knew it, the party was almost over. We just had to collect money from everyone and pay the bill.

"Is it free now?"

"Yup."

Izumi headed off to the bathroom as soon as Seno-san got back from using it. The people who had already paid and gotten ready to leave were sitting around chatting lazily or standing outside waiting for the rest of the group to leave. The mood was very chill.

Inside, Mimimi was hitting on Tama-chan by pretending she was still hungry and asking for a café date, while Nakamura and Mizusawa were messing around untying Takei's shoes. Same old, same old.

But just then, I witnessed something unusual.

"...Huh?"

Two girls were standing outside the bathroom—Hinami and Kikuchi-san.

"What's going on...?"

Those two didn't hang out much. And I don't think they were waiting for their turn in the bathroom—no, they seemed to be deep in discussion. About something pretty serious, too, from what I could tell.

My guess was they were continuing the slightly personal conversation Hinami had begun during the party. Still, it was unusual for Hinami to show her icier side to anyone but me.

A minute later, Izumi came out of the bathroom. She walked past Hinami and Kikuchi-san and headed to the table where I was standing to get her bag. When she got near, she glanced back at the two of them, apparently puzzled.

"Hey, Tomozaki, are they friends?"

"...Huh? Oh," I said, looking toward the bathroom again. "Yeah, that's not a pair I usually see together."

"Well, just now...," Izumi said, sounding worried.

"Yeah?"

"I overheard Kikuchi-san apologizing to Hinami." I could tell she was suspicious.

"Really?" That wasn't what I would've assumed. "Apologizing about what?"

"I don't know, but when I walked past, I heard her say, 'I'm sorry.' I didn't want to eavesdrop, so I came over here."

"...Oh."

It was unusual enough for the two of them to be talking, but for

Kikuchi-san to apologize…? I replayed the earlier conversation about the script in my mind, but I couldn't find anything specific worth apologizing for, so I just stood there, staring vaguely in their direction.

Eventually, Izumi said, "Oh, here they come."

"Yeah."

The conversation apparently over, they were walking toward us side by side. Hinami looked less serious now, and I didn't sense any tension.

"Is everyone ready to go?" she asked, looking at me and Izumi like nothing had happened.

"Uh, uh-huh." I nodded, swept along by her casual attitude.

"Should we go, then?" she replied before I had a chance to bring up any of my questions, and the four of us left the restaurant.

* * *

Outside, everyone was acting excited.

"Oooooh! It's snowing!"

Takei ran out into the street and waved his arms around.

"Snow…?"

Izumi and I exchanged glances. I stuck my hand out from under the eaves of the restaurant and sure enough.

"It really is snowing!" I stared at the flakes accumulating on my hand, surprised.

"Wait, it's really snow!" Izumi exclaimed happily, raising both hands toward the sky.

"Oh yeah…I think the weather report did call for snow."

Kikuchi-san and I both stood quietly, looking up at the dark Christmas Eve sky. Tiny white flakes danced through the air, glittering in the lights of the avenue as they drifted softly onto us.

"It's so beautiful," Hinami said, smiling. Her expression was gentle and full of a kind of all-embracing affection. As usual, I had no idea if it reflected her genuine feelings or if it was merely a mask. I hoped that at least in a moment like this she would let the world see her real emotions.

Kikuchi-san was still gazing up at the sky, her gloved hands held out palm up in front of her. Her expression was a tiny bit more childlike and naive than usual. After a moment, she captured a snowflake softly between her fingers.

"…Isn't it amazing?"

She laughed, her breath white, and looked up at me.

"Yeah." I nodded, smiling back at her.

We weren't on a date, but still, snow on my first Christmas with Kikuchi-san. Maybe it was pure coincidence, a random encounter in the game of life.

But for some reason, I felt like the whole world was wishing us well right then.

"A white Christmas," I mumbled, lost in the moment.

"It better stick! I wanna have a snowball fight! …Whoops!" Takei shouted, demolishing my quiet reverie as he slipped on a wet manhole cover and fell flat on his butt. "Man, that hurt!"

This guy really knows how to ruin the moment.

"Shut up, Takei."

"Geez, you're such a jerk sometimes!"

Which is why I told him exactly what I thought. He's convenient when the mood gets dark, but sometimes he's a total pest.

"So wanna go do karaoke now?" Nakamura suggested.

"Awesome idea! I'm in!" Takei answered, jumping right on board.

Then they looked at me and Kikuchi-san and grinned.

"You two are coming, too, right?"

"What, to karaoke?" I asked, caught off guard by this sudden development.

Nakamura nodded like it was totally obvious. "Yeah, right now."

"Um…," I hedged. I didn't have a reason to say no, and it might be fun to go since we were all hyper from the snow. But Kikuchi-san was standing next to me, and I didn't know if she would want to do something social. Actually, my guess was she wouldn't. And it wouldn't be right to leave her alone. As I was trying to decide what to do, Izumi interceded.

"Okay, Shuji, I'm sure we all want to go, but look at the time," she scolded.

"What?"

She held out her phone toward us. It was already ten o'clock. Incidentally, her home screen had a photo of a really busty foreign woman on it, which made me newly aware of how different our tastes are.

"I swear...you're such a killjoy."

"Am not! I just don't want to get in trouble!"

Arguing against the background of snow, they made me think of your stereotypical troublesome husband and virtuous wife. I wanted to tell them to go on like that for the rest of their lives. But Izumi was right—in Saitama, high school students are forbidden from being out in public after eleven at night. If you stay out past then, you get abducted by Kobaton, our prefectural mascot.

"Let's do it another time. I mean, since we'll be studying so hard next year, this is like our last winter break of high school," Mizusawa said, jumping in to smooth over the argument. Nakamura pouted silently for a second, then acquiesced to the inevitable.

"Okay, fine...I guess."

"What?! But it's snowing!" Meanwhile, Takei was still resisting, though his logic evaded me. "Wait, snow has nothing to do with karaoke."

"Nope...," Nakamura said, leaving Takei without a comeback. It's impossible to hate Takei because he gives in so easily when he's wrong.

I glanced at Kikuchi-san. Nakamura, Hinami, Izumi, and Mimimi were talking about when to do karaoke together. Would she want to go with them?

"What do you want to do?"

"Huh?"

"Do you want to go out to karaoke with them?" I whispered. She hesitated, then looked me in the eye.

"Um, I'm not the best in big groups...so I'd rather not."

She was turning down my invitation, but definitely not in a cold way.

"Okay," I said.

"But…I really like all of them, because they liked the play."

"Yeah," I said, smiling. It was important to respect her wishes. She wasn't rejecting them, she was carving out her own niche. She was simply saying that not everyone had to enjoy the same things.

"You should go with them and have fun," she said.

"You don't mind?"

She shook her head. "No. I mean, those are your good friends, right?"

"…Um, yeah."

It was embarrassing to be asked so directly, but I answered honestly.

"I want you to have a good time," she said, smiling cheerfully. "And tell me all about it afterward!" Her expression was radiant and her tone kind.

"Okay, I will."

Suddenly, a freezing cold something hit me in the face.

"…Oof!"

I spun around to find Takei laughing at me so hard I could practically see down his throat. I touched the cold substance on my face and clothes: snow. In other words…

"I'm gonna get you, asshole!" I shouted, glaring at him as I scraped up the snow that was starting to accumulate in colder corners of the street and packed it into a ball. You hit me; I'll pay you back with interest. I'm not just gonna lie down and take it. Such is the way of the gamer.

"Oh, so you wanna fight, Farm Boy?"

"I don't just play *Atafami*, you know. I play FPSs, too, and I've got good aim."

"Uh, I didn't get that, but you're in, right?"

Izumi was listening in on our ugly battle of words with dismay. "Guys are so immature!"

Kikuchi-san was watching from next to her, and she just giggled.

* * *

"Ha-ha…he got me good."

Fifteen minutes later, Kikuchi-san and I were standing under the eaves of a convenience store set back from the street down a short flight of stairs.

We'd just said good-bye to the group after a round of mortal combat between me and Takei—but now we were alone.

"Tee-hee. Yes, he did."

I hadn't been trying to get her alone. But after my defeat in the unexpected battle of snow scraped up from random crevices and corners, I'd been lured by a suspiciously smiley Mizusawa and Izumi over to the convenience store to buy hot chocolate, and now here we were. I'm fairly sure they ganged up on me so I'd make the most of this unusual white Christmas situation. I was cursing them silently for interfering—but yeah, I was happy to be alone with Kikuchi-san.

"Your friends are fun to hang out with," Kikuchi-san said.

"Huh? Oh, they just like to mess around…"

"…Yes, but they're still fun."

A puff of white breath escaped her lips as she giggled. She pressed one fluffy gloved hand to her mouth. Standing there in the snow on Minamiginza Street with its shops and restaurants, she looked both otherworldly and firmly planted in reality. I wasn't looking at an angel or a fairy—I was looking at a mystically beautiful human girl.

"So…should we head over to the station?"

"…Okay."

I took a step forward, matching my stride to hers. The downtown had that peaceful atmosphere it gets just before the new year, seasoned with the excitement of Christmas Eve. As the white flakes swirled more and more thickly from the sky, the streets began to look unfamiliar.

"Wow, I think it might actually stick," Kikuchi-san said.

"Yeah, maybe."

The snow melted on the asphalt, but it was slowly piling up on the seats of parked bicycles, the garbage cans next to vending machines, and the trees and bushes outside the station. At this rate, we might even wake up to a winter wonderland the next morning.

"We're alone together…on Christmas Eve."

"Um, uh, yeah."

I could feel my face instantly flush at this unexpectedly passionate statement from Kikuchi-san.

"I'm sorry, that was sudden… It's just—I feel so happy…"

"Oh yeah, of course. Um…so do I."

Our words were clumsy, but I'm sure they were honest.

We were a pair of lovers walking through the snowy city on a sacred night. Definitely a first for me, and a special one. Just walking along like that made me shy and happy and satisfied all at the same time.

"…There are so many people out tonight," Kikuchi-san said.

"Yeah."

Christmas music drifted from every shop and restaurant, and I'm not sure, but there seemed to be an unusually large number of couples among the crowd. In the past, that kind of thing always made me feel lonely, but tonight, their excitement was contagious. Maybe that's why even a bottom-tier character like me had the urge to implement the idea that suddenly popped into my head.

"Um, can you wait a second?"

I scraped up some of the snow that had settled on the bushes and trees and began to shape it between my hands. I was being a little more careful than earlier when I made snowballs to throw at Takei.

"Tomozaki-kun?"

The idea had come to me as the two of us were walking through this holy night. True, we'd only been dating for two days, so maybe it was inevitable that I wasn't prepared. Still, not having anything to give her made me sad. So I gathered up the snow and formed it into two little balls, smaller than the palm of my hand. Kikuchi-san must have known by then what I was up to. Since I had the snowball fight to thank for the idea, I had to admit that maybe I should be grateful for Takei's existence for the first time in my life. I placed one of the balls on top of the other on my palm and held it out to Kikuchi-san.

"Um, h-here's your Christmas present…?"

I didn't have much confidence in that statement.

The misshapen little creation sat on the tips of my fingers. It didn't have a nose or eyes or mouth, but it was identifiably a snowman. At least the bottom part was bigger than the top one. Kikuchi-san stared at it, and after a few seconds, a chuckle escaped her lips. She picked it up and set it

on her own hand. Then she beckoned for me to follow and squatted down next to the base of a tree.

"Let's put these on it."

She took off her gloves and picked up something from the ground that looked like a seed. An innocent, happy smile on her face, she pressed two of them onto the snowman.

"Oh, they're eyes."

"Tee-hee. Yes!"

Now the grotesque little snowman had one big eye and one small one, which made it look even more homemade. It was such a ridiculously amateurish job that as I stared at it, I wanted to laugh.

"That's the ugliest snowman I've ever seen!"

"But he's so cute!"

"...He is."

We look at each other and burst out laughing. Even though we were just being silly together, that brief moment in time felt immeasurably precious.

"...Um, so...," I said, getting my nerve up to make a proposal. "Want to take a photo with it?"

I wanted to preserve this moment forever.

"Yes!" she answered, bowling me over with her excitement.

"Great! So..." With the camera skills I learned during my Instagram assignment, I swiftly prepared to shoot the photo. "Okay, ready!"

"Okay!"

I snapped the three of us together: me, Kikuchi-san, and the snowman.

"...Whew, not blurry."

"...What?"

For a second, Kikuchi-san seemed confused by my comment, not realizing that blurry photos are my norm. But that was fine. The important thing was that I got the picture.

"I'll send it to you later," I said.

"Yes, please do!"

We started walking toward the station again.

"Oh dear, I don't think they'll let him on the train," she said regretfully.

"Ah-ha-ha. Sad but true."

Succumbing to inevitable reality, we set the snowman down on the roots of a tree. We glanced at each other, then both waved good-bye.

A moment later, we were at Omiya Station, and our time together was over.

"Oh, um...," Kikuchi-san said in a determined tone. She was looking up at me with moist eyes. "When can I see you again...?"

"Um..."

Her voice and expression were much warmer than when we were around other people.

"Next time...I want to go out just the two of us...like we are right now."

Her expression was expectant, like she was counting on me for something. An ordinary glance from her was enough to make me blush, so needless to say, this particular expression turned me into a tongue-tied idiot.

"Uh, um...w-wait a second."

My heart melting beneath her gaze, I pulled up the calendar on my phone and searched for a free day soon. I wanted to see her again as much as she wanted to see me.

"...How about the day after tomorrow or the day after that?"

"Oh, okay, then the day after tomorrow!"

She latched on to my suggestion in an excited, almost anxious way.

"Ah-ha-ha, got it." Then I realized something. "...Oh."

Kikuchi-san tilted her head quizzically. As for what I'd noticed when I looked at the calendar...

"I'm free on New Year's Day..." I tried to say it as casually and confidently as possible. I mean, this was what I wanted, after all. "Want to go to a shrine together?"

"Oh, I'd love to!" she said right away, nodding enthusiastically.

"Ah-ha-ha... So we'll skip the day after tomorrow and get together on New Year's?" I said, figuring I'd better not monopolize too much of her time. She caught her breath, instantly crestfallen.

"What's wrong?"

"It's just that…" She paused for a moment, searching for words before finally looking up at me with those moist eyes, her cheeks flushed. "…I want to see you on both days."

Definitely not fair. How was I supposed to even think when she said something like that?

"O-okay, then both. Let's meet both times," I said, surrendering my heart completely.

"…Okay. I'm glad," she said, lowering her head.

"Uh…me too."

We were awkward, but we were sharing our feelings. Simply arranging our next date turned me into a quivering mess. The world right then truly was filled with color. I couldn't help thinking that the photo we took, along with the memory of this moment, was the best Christmas present I could have hoped for.

* * *

We went through the ticket gate together. Since we live on different train lines, this was where we would part ways.

"Well…I'll get in touch soon."

"O-okay."

My heart still thumping, I watched her walk away, then headed to the Saikyo Line platform. Images from earlier in the day were flickering through my mind. I felt light and happy—but also a little bit lonely.

I walked down the stairs to the platform and glanced at the timetable. My train was scheduled to leave in a few minutes.

I was still floating on air when it arrived and I stepped aboard. As the train began to move, I looked out at the snowy city streets. Suddenly, I remembered something Izumi had said.

"I overheard Kikuchi-san apologizing to Hinami."

I never did get a chance to ask Kikuchi-san what the two of them had been talking about. I hadn't wanted to ruin the moment, but really, I felt like it wasn't my business.

Soon the train pulled into Kitayono Station. I left the station and was walking slowly toward my house when—

"Ah!"

A notification buzzed on my phone. I took it out of my pocket and saw that it was a LINE message from Kikuchi-san. I opened the chat window right away.

[*Thank you for today.*
I'm not sure why, but I felt so happy and relaxed. It was really fun.]

[*When we were talking, and when we made our next date...*
I realized we really are together, and my heart was pounding so hard. I'm so looking forward to seeing you the day after tomorrow and on New Year's Day.]

I felt like I was about to collapse to the ground in a dead faint just from reading it. So unfair!

"—Erg!"

The streets of Kitayono were chilly, but the message from Kikuchi-san and the photo we'd taken together felt hotter than a hand warmer in my palm.

2

A nameless flower

Bottom-
Tier
CHARACTER
TOMOZAKI

"Kaboom!"

"Nooo! You tricked me, Aoi!"

"I did not!"

Innocent voices called back and forth in a small children's room. Three elementary-aged girls were sitting in front of a TV set hooked up to an old game console. On the screen, two pixel-art pigs wearing sunglasses raced around shooting each other with laser guns. Aoi and Nagisa were playing while Haruka, the shortest of the three, watched.

"Hya!" Aoi said as she nimbly moved her fingers on the controller. Oinko, her pig character, swiftly dodged a bomb and aimed an energy blast at Nagisa, hitting her target perfectly.

"Ahhhhh!! Nagisa got hit!" her younger sister Haruka squealed.

"Hee-hee, you're easy to beat!" Aoi set her controller down and gloated at her sister.

"Darn it, I lost…" Nagisa pouted and stared at her controller for a second, then turned to Aoi and said cheerfully, "Let's play again!"

"Really? You're just gonna lose again."

"Will not! I'm gonna win this time!" Nagisa announced confidently, though she had no reason for it. She gripped her controller and stared straight at the screen.

"Ugh. If I have to," Aoi said, intentionally kindling her sister's competitiveness. She grabbed her controller with a relaxed expression as Haruka watched excitedly.

"Get her good, Nagisa! Down with Aoi the Evil Overlord!"

"Leave it to me!"

"Hey, why'm I the Evil Overlord?!" Aoi asked, laughing.

The game started, and her fingers flickered nimbly over the controller.

"Ooh...she's so good."

The two pigs on the screen clashed, shooting, dodging, and chipping away at each other. At the same moment as in the last game, Nagisa threw a bomb. Aoi dodged it and fired at Nagisa in the lag.

"Heh-heh, that's all you've got?"

This time, Nagisa grinned boldly.

"Nope... Gotcha!"

"Oh no!"

Just before Aoi's blast hit, Nagisa launched a second bomb. It canceled out Aoi's blast, then barreled straight into Oinko.

"Ahhhh!"

The bomb exploded into Oinko, who instantly vanished. A moment later, the results screen appeared.

"That's so correct, I think I've been hexed!!" Nagisa's Oinko—a different color from Aoi's—said, striking a pose.

"Yesss! See that? I won!"

"Wow, you're super good!" Haruka said.

"Thanks for cheering for me, Haruka!"

"*Sniff, sniff...*"

Aoi scrunched up her eyebrows dramatically, whimpering like a baby. Nagisa pounced on her, grinning.

"Oof!"

"Hey, Nagisa, be careful!" Aoi said, wrapping her arms around her younger sister and tapping her back with a wry smile.

"Aoi!"

"What?"

Nagisa grinned from ear to ear, still in Aoi's arms, and announced, "This is fun!"

Her words were so honest and direct that Aoi grinned back and answered, "Yeah, I know!" And even though she'd just lost, she really, truly meant it.

* * *

"Agh."

The Sekitomo School Festival Celebration and Christmas Party was over, and Aoi Hinami was on her way home. Her mind was full of old memories. She was thinking about the days when Nagisa and Haruka were both still there, when their little room still felt huge. As the train rocked along through the night, her thoughts, for once, were stuck in the past.

Of course, she knew why that was—for one, the play Fuka Kikuchi had written, and for another, the conversation they'd had at the party earlier that night. More specifically, the emotions depicted in the play and the words Fuka had said to her. Unsettling, long-buried memories were slowly rising to the surface.

Outside the train windows, snow fell heavily. It was slowly covering the bare face of the city with a beautiful, pure white layer, like a mask. Aoi gazed out at the darkened city. Or perhaps she was searching for her own faint reflection in the window.

"...It doesn't matter," she muttered to herself, steadying her breath. She sounded as if she were announcing this fact to the world. Whichever it was, she tossed her words out violently, with an unusually steely strength.

Another memory had risen to the surface.

A memory of defeat and determination.

* * *

It was early summer. Aoi was in her third year of junior high, and her hard work was starting to yield satisfying results—yet she was unsure how to move forward.

"Well done! First place again," said her homeroom teacher, a man in his midforties, as he handed Aoi an A4-size sheet of paper with her grades. He was smiling proudly, almost as if the achievement were his own.

"Ah-ha-ha. Thank you. I hope I can do as well next time."

Aoi made sure her smile was soft as she took the paper from him. Her scores in each subject were written in a column, with "1/154" at the very bottom. She attended a public junior high on the outskirts of Omiya. The number meant she'd achieved the highest final exam score in her grade. It was an objective, straightforward affirmation of her path.

"You've got plenty of rivals. Don't slack off."

"I know. I'll keep studying hard."

She rearranged her expression to signal renewed commitment. But the truth was, she was almost certain she would get the top score again. She'd already gotten it three times in a row. She knew how to do it; as long as she stayed consistent, she figured she could repeat her success.

"After all, I've set a pattern now."

Until her first year of junior high, her grades had been average—actually, they'd fluctuated between average and below average. Over time, she'd gradually pushed them up, until she finally reached the summit with her first-place score. Her efforts might not be visible, but they were firmly rooted in her as something she could reproduce.

"I'll do my best to keep it up."

"Good. I'm expecting you to go far," her teacher said.

Problem was, now that she knew she could keep getting the same results, she was gradually losing interest in doing so.

"...Keep it up...," she mumbled.

"What was that, Hinami?"

"Oh, nothing. Thank you so much."

After all, she could prove herself no further in this particular arena.

* * *

At six thirty that evening, Aoi was on the basketball court in the gym. She stood confidently in front of two rows of players, an intense expression on her face.

"All right, that's it for today. The tournament is coming up, so be careful not to injure yourself, everyone."

She smiled, then swept her gaze over the players one by one, looking each one in the face. She was captain of the team. All thirty or so members looked back at her solemnly, and a slight shudder of tension ran through them as their eyes met hers. She had created this atmosphere entirely on her own.

She smiled at them in satisfaction, then relaxed her expression theatrically.

"…Thanks, ladies, for coming on this journey with me."

"Aoi…?"

Chinami Yokoyama, the assistant captain, was standing in the middle of the lines of players. She glanced at Aoi in surprise, thrown off by her sudden swing from cold to warm.

"Yes, well…I know the tournament is still a month away, but I wanted to say something now."

Aoi looked down, peeked at everyone bashfully, then raised her head again.

"I know I've been tough on you the past year or two, and maybe I've been a little selfish. I've worked you hard during practice, and I've set impossible goals."

"That's not—"

"No," she said, cutting Yokoyama off but in a kind tone. "I'm truly grateful to you all."

She slowly bent down, picked up the basketball at her feet, and dribbled it in front of her. The rhythmic sound echoed across the court to the players. Then she caught the ball affectionately in her arms, and silence returned to the court. All eyes were trained on her. She knew that repetitive movement and sound was a good way of drawing their attention.

"At first, I wasn't sure."

"…You weren't?"

This uncharacteristic display of weakness further drew out her teammates' emotions.

"To tell the truth…I thought people would say I was crazy for thinking our team could make it to the nationals, when we'd only ever gotten to the prefectural finals before."

Aoi was faltering on purpose, so the revelation would feel less intentional and more real.

"But you know what? You believed in me. You believed I was serious."

She put on her bashful face again, but this time, she infused her expression with a tiny bit more emotion and gratitude.

"I would have given up a long time ago if it wasn't for all of you."

Her expression looked fragile enough to crumple any second, and her gestures were warm and affectionate. The two lines of players caught their breath at her words, and soon they were stumbling over themselves to reply.

"But...that's only because you worked harder than any of us!"

"Yeah! If it weren't for you, we would never have made it this far!"

"Exactly! I'm so...happy I'm on the...b-b-basketball team with you, Hinami!"

The emotions were spilling forth now, and some of the girls had started to cry. Aoi took in the sight of her team with a smile on her face as she slowly nodded. She turned away for a second and wiped at her eyes. When she looked back at them, all trace of tears was gone.

She made eye contact with Yokoyama and gently tossed her the ball. Yokoyama grabbed it firmly.

"I said I couldn't have made it this far without you...but this isn't the end. I'll need you in the future, too."

She met Yokoyama's eyes again and held her arms out at chest level. Yokoyama tossed her the ball, and she caught it with both hands. Next, she passed it to a second-year student named Kagami.

"We can't make it to first place unless everyone works together."

"...First place?"

She'd said the words casually, but which *first place* did she mean? Her teammates knew the words, but they didn't sense her true meaning yet.

Aoi held her arms out, and Kagami passed the ball back to her. Their actions were almost ceremonial. After all, Aoi had planned out every moment of this performance.

"I'm serious." She put her hand in the right pocket of her sweat suit. "Do you know what this is?"

She pulled out a slip of paper. Everyone leaned forward to see what it was, then exchanged glances.

"Um..."

When she sensed no one was going to answer, Aoi continued speaking in a casual tone.

"It's my report card. We got our scores on finals today, right?" She looked at Yokoyama. "Yoko-chan, I wasn't a very good student in our first year, was I?"

"Um…no, you weren't," Yokoyama said. She didn't know the details of Aoi's grades, but her image of Aoi back then was not as a star student.

"But I worked little by little to improve…and now I'm in first place."

She was gazing out confidently at her teammates. Yokoyama already knew she'd gotten first again, so she wasn't surprised, but she was filled with renewed admiration.

"This is your third time in a row to be first, isn't it?"

Their teammates gasped. Aoi nodded, satisfied with their response, and tucked the paper back into her pocket without unfolding it.

"I'm not trying to boast… I just want you to believe in me."

She didn't think they actively doubted her, but she did feel their faith was slightly short of what was needed for them to bet on her—so she continued speaking slowly, lighting a fire in their hearts.

"I'm first in our school—but only in our school. I got there by tackling my weaknesses… And I think this team can do the same."

Perhaps because they guessed what she was going to say next, their attention was drawn increasingly to her words and expression.

"You've always been good players, and you worked hard for the past two years. We came together as a team to achieve our shared goal."

All eyes were glued to her.

"That's why I know we can reach any heights we shoot for."

She made sure her tone was powerful and earnest.

"Let's do this! Let's shoot for the stars!"

In unison, her teammates responded: "Yeah!"

Some of them were crying, and others looked determined. Each expression was slightly different, but they all believed in her fully.

Sensing that they were all aligned behind the same goal now, she nodded once, firmly. Partly, she was satisfied because everyone was fired up to go to nationals. But more than that, she was pleased that *the speech she had practiced over and over* had had its intended effect on her teammates. That in itself was gratifying.

She might have been expecting this—expecting that she would be able to prove herself in this new arena.

* * *

Aoi walked to the station with the rest of the team, then split off and headed home by herself. In the entryway, she slipped off her loafers and paused in front of the closed living room door. She could hear her mother moving around on the other side. Oil was sizzling in the kitchen; apparently, she was frying something. Her mother's presence unsettled her just slightly.

Aoi placed her hand on her chest, then reached into her pocket and fingered her report card. As she reached for the doorknob, she visualized her mother's happy reaction and her own response.

"...I'm home!" she called innocently and turned the knob. As she'd guessed, her mother was standing in the kitchen cooking. She smiled brightly at her daughter.

"Hi, Aoi! Good timing."

"For what?"

"Dinner's almost ready. I made cheeseburgers, your favorite."

"Yay! Thank you!"

Her demeanor now was intentionally a bit more girlish than when she was in school. She took her usual spot at the dining table. Her mother set a lid on the frying pan and sat down across from Aoi.

"Is dinner okay?" Aoi asked.

"Yes, it's fine. I always put a lid on at the end to let the burgers finish cooking after I turn off the heat. It's a little trick to make the meat more tender."

"Wow!" Aoi said, overacting just a bit.

Her mother smiled. "How's school going?" she asked casually.

Aoi stiffened; she was about to affirm her own achievement.

"...Well, we got our test scores back today," she replied, pretending to have just remembered.

"How'd you do?"

It was an ordinary question, but before she answered, Aoi made sure her expression was slightly playful and her tone relaxed.

"Can you believe it? I got first again."

"Really? That's wonderful!" her mother cheered. She nodded with satisfaction, then smiled kindly. "You really are my little indigo flower, always blooming and reaching for the sun."

Aoi was a bit surprised by her mother's reaction, and for a second, she didn't know what to say. But she quickly pasted a smile back on her face.

"...Aren't I?"

"You sure are. I'm always bragging to the other moms about you."

"Ah-ha-ha. Now you're buttering me up."

Her mother's happiness and unconditional approval didn't come as a surprise. They talked for a few more minutes, then her mother stood up to check on their dinner. Aoi let out a long breath and bit her lip at her own weakness. Her mother slid the hamburgers onto their plates.

"Can you go tell Haruka dinner is ready?"

"Sure."

Aoi walked upstairs to her sister's room. She was three years younger, a sixth grader in elementary school.

"Haruka?" she called, knocking on the door.

"Wait a second!" came the excited response. Aoi could make out the faint sound of video game background music on the other side of the door.

"Dinner's ready."

"Okay, I'll come down as soon as this game's over!"

"All righty," Aoi said, smiling wryly as she walked back downstairs and sat at the table again. Her mother was in the kitchen putting the finishing touches on their three plates.

"Where's your sister?"

"Playing a video game. She said she'll come down when she's done."

"She's really obsessed with that game," her mother said with a giggle as she carried their plates to the table.

"I know. I think it's called *Attack Families*?"

"Yep."

"It's super popular right now. All the boys in my class are into it."

Aoi's mother sat down across from her to wait for Haruka.

"You're not interested?"

"I'm not sure I have time to play video games."

"Ah-ha-ha. True, you've got homework and basketball already, so adding in games probably *would* be a bit much."

"...Yeah."

Her mother's response made her a little uneasy, but they kept on talking. A few minutes later, Haruka came downstairs. "Ooh, hamburgers!"

"With cheese!" their mother said proudly.

"Yum! Your favorite, right, Aoi?"

Aoi smiled at her sister's childish reaction, as if it reassured her.

"Yup. Hurry up and sit down, okay?"

Once they were all seated, they began their meal. It was an ordinary, peaceful family scene. But there was something anxious and unsettled in Aoi's expression, as if she hadn't yet fully defined herself.

* * *

After dinner, Aoi went to her room and opened the Excel file she filled in every day on her computer. A graph showing her quiz and test scores over time was pulled up on the screen. The line started out nearly flat before curving up at an increasingly steep angle, eventually zooming to the top. The shape reflected not only her first-place status but also her growing ROI on the effort she'd been putting in. Essentially, she was learning to put in "the right kind of effort."

"Okay...okay."

She took a deep breath, let it out, and gazed at the graph with something verging on excitement. Was she gazing at the present, the path she took to get there, or the future? Whatever the answer, the uncertainty of earlier had vanished from her face.

"...Let's see."

She opened a Word file and began to edit it. The heading read *"Midterm Goals,"* with a list of phrases below: *"Stay in first place on finals and* midterms," "*Become a top basketball player and lead the team to nationals,*" "*Become a central member of the most popular group.*"

Her fingers reached down to the mouse pad below the keyboard. As she ran her fingers over it, the cursor on the screen selected the text, turning the background black. Aoi stared at the screen for a moment, then lightly pressed a key. Instantly, the three lines of text disappeared. All that remained was the heading, with an expanse of white below. Each vision and goal she achieved left emptiness in its wake. A meaningless column.

"Okay."

She took another deep breath, thinking in order to control her anxiety. As long as she was running, everything was easy, but the second she stopped, she was drenched in sweat. She was already growing accustomed to a state of constant running.

She had reached first place in her school in several arenas—in her midterms and finals, the arena of academics; among her classmates, the arena of communication; and on the basketball team, the arena of physical ability. So what was her next goal?

She nodded and began to type, recalling the scene at practice earlier that day. She wanted those results to be reproducible. In which case, she needed a new arena. Something she hadn't achieved yet.

"*Win first place in the basketball nationals.*"

She stared at this new promise to herself, then closed the Word file, satisfied.

* * *

A month passed.

"We can do this! We've made it this far; we can finish it off!"

Aoi and her team had won the prefectural tournament without incident and were now at nationals. Their school hadn't been on anyone's radar, and now here they were facing off with the nation's best. That should have been more than enough to satisfy anyone, though it was the inevitable outcome of the amount and quality of effort they'd put in. At least in the realm of junior high sports, Aoi had polished her method to an art.

"For sure! Don't let up now, ladies! Work your magic!"

"Ah-ha-ha. Come on, Yokoyama—that's Aoi's line."

"Hey, let me have this!"

Everyone on the team had worked hard to reach this moment. They stood next to the court, supporting one another as they revved themselves up for the game.

"Let's go!"

Their battle for the national title was about to start.

Two days later, Aoi stood on the court crying.

She'd made it to the national tournament, where the best teams from all over Japan fought it out on the main stage. But her team came in second.

Needless to say, Aoi was not crying tears of joy. She was frustrated at being only the second best in the whole country.

By any other standards, the team's results would have been too good to be true. Until a year earlier, they'd have been lucky to make it to the prefectural tournament, and now suddenly they were the second-best team in Japan. They hadn't managed to capture the gold medal, but anyone would have been amazed by their achievement. And Aoi was the one who got them there. No one would dream of criticizing her.

But still.

"First place goes to Yatsuyanagi Junior High School."

At the closing ceremony, Aoi gritted her teeth hearing the words *first place* paired with the name of a school that was not her own. Her frustration at her results, as incredible as they were, was so overwhelming she felt it was ripping her apart. Perhaps the tears stemmed from all the determination and effort she'd put in, or perhaps from a sense that she was under a spell she couldn't escape.

"..."

Standing next to her, Yokoyama silently rested a hand on Aoi's

shoulder. But she couldn't bring herself to even murmur Aoi's name. She had realized something as she watched her team captain sob. Like the others, Yokoyama had worked harder in the past year than she ever imagined she could work. She'd followed Aoi's lead, walking in her shadow—perhaps to grant Aoi's wish.

But Aoi always worked much harder.

A thought lurked in the back of Yokoyama's mind—and in the minds of all the other girls on the team.

If there were five Aois on the team, we would have won.

That's why she and the others remained silent. They'd followed her, but the dream of being the top team in Japan was a dream that Aoi gave them, no more. It had never been something they themselves were determined to achieve.

"…!"

Yokoyama bit her lip, frustrated at her own dependence and powerlessness. But realizing that now didn't help the situation. She couldn't rewind time, and she couldn't reverse the tournament results.

They'd always depended on Aoi when they were in trouble, even in basketball games. She became their go-to in difficult situations. Eventually, they started believing they wouldn't reach their dream through their own efforts, but that Aoi would lead them there.

"…I'm fine, Yoko-chan…"

That's why Yokoyama and the other players didn't comfort her or congratulate one another on their hard work.

In fact, they couldn't even feel genuine regret over the outcome.

* * *

A few hours later, the team was in a room at a Japanese restaurant in Omiya that their coach had rented out for a party. The tension of the game had dissipated, and all thirty team members, including the reserve players and first-year students, were gathered in the large tatami room.

"Thanks for all your hard work, Aoi!"

"You looked awesome out there!"

"It's so amazing we got second place…!"

The words of congratulation and praise that the younger players offered soothed Aoi slightly, but of course they didn't reach her core. Not a single person in the room had worked as hard as her; they couldn't genuinely praise her, and she couldn't genuinely praise them.

"Ah-ha-ha. Thanks."

The best she could do was nod and smile superficially.

As the party was winding down, the starters each said a few words to the group before everyone went home. The five girls stood in front of the others, while the rest of the team watched attentively.

"I've never worked so hard for anything in my whole life…! It's all thanks to Aoi…!"

Each speech was full of praise and gratitude for her.

"I'm so happy I was able to be on this team with…Aoi…and the rest of you!"

Their words were tearful but positive. That honesty gradually began to have an effect on Aoi, reaching the soft parts of her that she hadn't yet molded to perfection. She held back the wave of emotion rising within her, staring straight ahead. The other four starters finished their short speeches, and now it was her turn. She had naturally gone last, and with her speech, the curtain would fall on their entire basketball team experience. Everyone was waiting eagerly for her words. She slowly opened her mouth.

"…Ladies, thank you for this year."

She was struggling to make this speech, doing her best to wear the proper mask of a basketball team captain.

"I was only able to work this hard because all of you came together."

Writhing beneath her own painful regret, she desperately searched for the ideal words.

"I don't think I could have done it with any other team. No one else would have believed enough to make this fairy tale come true."

She had to complete her role in perfection.

"We fell just a tiny bit short of our goal, but second place is incredible, right?"

She had to prove her own rightness one more time.

"Being on the team with all of you this year…"

But as she prepared to conclude her speech, a strange, dark tentacle of emotion slithered over her mind.

"Being on the team…has been…"

The words caught in her throat as the murky feeling pushed up from deep inside her, threatening to overflow. All she had to do was say those beautiful, ideal words, just like everyone else. That was all she had to do to put a neat, tidy bow on this long, long role she'd poured herself into over the past year as captain of the Kusunoki Junior High basketball team.

But she couldn't finish the sentence.

"It's been…"

She was not able to share the same emotion as everybody else. They'd *lost*. They hadn't achieved their goal. She could not honestly say that she enjoyed her time on the team, not by any definition.

Little by little, she sensed her emotions and thoughts spinning beyond her control.

"…"

She realized something then. Her eye had always been on something different from everyone else. She knew that she could not go back to the person she had once been. She was fundamentally different from everyone else—there was no one with whom she could share her outlook on the world.

She realized that large tears were rolling down her cheeks. She herself didn't understand exactly why she was crying. All she knew was that she felt horribly, terribly alone in the world.

"Aoi…?"

The younger girls were starting to cry, too. Needless to say, they had no idea what was going on inside her at all. But they trusted her so deeply that the mere sight of her crying was enough to bring them to tears.

However.

"…Aoi."

The starters felt something slightly different. Aoi was crying tears of frustration during her speech, but her eyes held no hint of weakness. She stared straight ahead so fixedly it was as if she couldn't do anything else. She took full responsibility for everything she had taken on—and she existed on an entirely different plane from them.

Her power was understated but also completely unnatural.

For the first time, the starters were a bit frightened of her. It was the first time she had exposed herself to them. But the hidden part of herself that she had exposed, the part beneath the armor of her performance, was grotesquely strong.

"So, everybody... Thank you!"

In the end, she finished her speech without saying the words she had set out to say.

* * *

Late that night, Aoi sat gazing vacantly at her computer screen. Beneath the heading *"Midterm Goals"* was the line of text reading *"Win first place in the basketball nationals."* She had selected the text, and her finger was hovering above the DELETE button.

"...!"

She was so used to setting and renewing her goals that it had almost become a routine. Still, in that moment, something within her resisted pushing the button. Pushing it was the most humiliating thing she could imagine. It was her first decisive defeat.

How could she possibly be erasing a goal *because she hadn't achieved it?*

Aoi bit her lip and managed to prevent the central pillar in her heart from collapsing—and tapped the button. The sound seemed to echo through the room like an explosion. The joint of the finger she'd used to press the button throbbed slightly. The words were finally gone, leaving a white space. Her own emptiness materialized before her eyes. What would she fill it with?

"Aoi?"

Suddenly, she heard a voice calling from outside her door. She took a breath and answered.

"Haruka, is that you?"

"I was wondering..."

"...What?"

Haruka's answer was something Aoi could never have imagined. "...Do you wanna play a video game?"

"Huh?"

She was surprised. Haruka hadn't asked her to do something like that in a long time. Until a few years earlier, the three of them had often played together, but ever since that day, the sisters had almost never played video games. Aoi figured it was because she had begun to focus with such maniacal intensity on her goals. Or maybe it was because retracing similar memories would lead her to remember the brilliance of that day, and so she instinctively shrank from it. Anyway, it was unusual for Haruka to invite her like this.

"Come on, play *Atafami* with me!"

* * *

"N-no way..."

"Crushed you!"

The game's real name was *Attack Families*, but everyone called it *Atafami*. It was the most popular PvP action game in Japan.

Aoi and Haruka were sitting in front of the TV in the living room, each holding a controller. Aoi wasn't sure why Haruka had suddenly invited her to play, but she guessed it might have been an attempt to cheer her up. That didn't mean she was going easy on Aoi, of course—really, she was as intent on winning as she always had been when the three of them played.

"Oof..."

Aoi stared at the results screen in a daze. Back when the three of them were all crazy about games for no particular reason, Aoi had been the best player. Even though she'd only played *Atafami* once or twice before, she never expected Haruka to beat her with three out of four stocks left.

"I can't believe I lost so badly to a sixth grader!"

"You haven't practiced enough."

"L-let's go again!"

"Sure!"

But the results weren't any different from their first game. Her relative lack of experience with *Atafami* was entirely to blame, but still, Aoi couldn't help feeling disgruntled.

"Argh, damn it!"

"You had that coming!"

"What!! Why couldn't I hit you?"

"It's called a spot dodge."

"I-I've never heard of that…"

The battle was lopsided but heated. The third-year junior high student getting trounced by the sixth-year elementary student seemed somehow younger than she was and fully invested in the game.

"I l-lost again…"

"That was easy! I think you studied too much and now you're bad at games."

"Grrr…"

Aoi glared at her little sister. Of course, both of them were still children. But Aoi had always hated to lose. Being crushed this badly was incredibly frustrating for her.

Maybe because they were so excited and wrapped up in the game, they didn't notice their mother standing behind them. A soapy sponge in one hand, she was watching them in a trance.

"Oh, Mom!" Aoi said when she finally noticed her there. She felt oddly embarrassed, as if her mother had caught her doing something bad. But her mother smiled, her eyes sparkling, and said something Aoi hadn't expected.

"…You look like you're really having fun, Aoi."

"Huh?"

Aoi was genuinely surprised by her mother's words. She was losing game after game to her younger sister—but she was having fun? For Aoi, who had spent the past several years constantly pursuing victory and eventually found herself unable to even utter the word *fun*, her mother's comment felt very unnatural.

But her mother wasn't the only one with that impression. Haruka was smiling innocently at her, too.

"You really do!"

Aoi loved that smile of Haruka's—and it made her a little shy. She started to feel unsure. How did she really feel, inside the mask, in her innermost heart? What expression was her real self making? Was she genuinely *enjoying* her recent loss? She looked down at the controller in her hands, feeling oddly unsettled.

"...Do I?"

The uncharacteristically uncertain question was directed at herself.

* * *

After that, Aoi started playing *Atafami* with Haruka on a regular basis. Was she simply trying to get better at the game? Or was she drawn to that emotion she'd felt for a fleeting moment? Whichever the answer, she got more and more obsessed.

"Hmm...so you figured out that I always jump here..."

She had a habit of sorts. Whenever she was faced with something that had rules and results, she unconsciously began to analyze its structure. She did it with schoolwork and club activities and even with the structure of relationships in her class. In the process of aiming for the top, she'd become better than anyone else at analyzing these systems. Of course, she quickly surpassed Haruka at *Atafami*.

"Eek! Aoi, you really are the Evil Overlord!"

The strange thing was, no matter how many times she played *Atafami* with Haruka, that was the only time that excitement welled up inside her.

"Heh-heh! I won!"

"You're too good! How'd you get so good?"

"I'm just a natural, I guess."

True, she'd beaten Haruka. But that alive, warm feeling didn't come from winning.

"Haruka?! No fair..."

"Is too fair!"

"Ooh, if I run this way, you'll fall off the edge and I won't."

"Hey! Now you're being unfair!"

"Ah-ha-ha. Am not."

The mood was a lot like it had been when the three sisters had played together years ago.

"Aoi?"

"What?"

The rowdy game over, Haruka gently set down her controller.

"We used to play games like this a lot...before."

"...I know."

The expression on Haruka's face was a mixture of sadness and loneliness. Aoi didn't need to ask to know what she meant. She ruffled her sister's hair affectionately. If she hadn't, she felt sure the loneliness would have overtaken her, too.

"...Okay, Haruka! Let's play one more time!"

"What, really? You haven't had enough yet?"

Maybe the two of them were running from the loneliness, or maybe they were indulging in the nostalgia. They played again and again and again. Three controllers were plugged into the console. But the sister who used to hold the third one was no longer there.

* * *

Before she knew it, Aoi was more obsessed with *Atafami* than Haruka was. When Haruka was home, she played with her sister, and when she wasn't, she played online. It was as if she'd found her place. Any game might have served the same purpose, as long as she and Haruka could laugh together as they played. As long as it uncovered their buried memories and feelings from that other time, anything would have done—maybe it didn't even have to be a video game.

But by chance, *Atafami* also happened to fit Hinami's criteria for the best games. The correct type of effort yielded the correct results, without unfair flukes or inequalities. Simple rules entwined in a complex way to form a deeply engaging game. In other words, a god-tier game.

Each time she dove into it, she felt more convinced that it was as interesting as real life. Plus, it had the most players of any PvP game in Japan, so anytime she went online, she could play against other high-level players from all over the country. She could even tell how good they were from their winrates. Aoi believed only in numbers and results, and attaining them was everything to her. There could hardly be a more perfect way to fill the emptiness in her heart.

Within several months of getting into *Atafami*, her winrate had rocketed to the top 0.5 percent, making her inarguably one of the best players in the country. That was when she realized something.

Ever since the day she decided to do things right, ever since the moment she realized she needed to win more than anyone else, she thought she had taken the best course of action. But she had lost the basketball tournament. Now she knew why.

"..."

No, she had probably known it since the moment she lost. Maybe she had begun to sense it even earlier, when she was practicing with the team. She knew why she hadn't won.

Because she hadn't been pursuing a personal goal.

Of course, managing other people's motivations could be inherent to winning, in a sense. But ultimately, other people were other people. Controlling them completely was impossible. She suspected that her teammates had sensed the same thing. They pushed themselves to the limit for her, but they still couldn't be like her. They lacked the same driving force, the same emptiness.

She couldn't blame them for it. She was simply a different kind of person than they were.

Aoi stayed in her room playing *Atafami* like a girl possessed. Her handle was Aoi. She didn't have a good reason for making that her name, beyond the fact that it was the name she'd registered her console under. She hadn't felt the need to choose a special name, and a common name like Aoi seemed just right for diving single-mindedly into competitions.

The most important thing was playing *Atafami* constantly helped her relieve her regrets slightly. The way that her effort was instantly reflected in her winrate suited her personality perfectly. It was a way to prove her impeccable correctness.

"…Whoa, seriously?"

One day, she was paired with a new opponent and felt a jolt of surprise. She knew that name. At first, she thought her opponent must be an impostor, but when she saw the number written next to the name, she knew it really was him.

nanashi   Winrate: 2,569

That number was incredible. *Of course* she knew the name. She was going up against the best player in Japan, the one who had consistently held onto the top winrate. Nanashi.

"…Yes!"

A quiet joy bubbled up inside her. She'd been wanting to play him forever. Gender and age didn't matter in this simple, fair, incredible game. This was the top *Atafami* player in Japan, who had built up an incredible record. In the world of gaming, he was a monster who did everything right.

Even though they were playing online, this was still an opportunity to face off against someone truly worthy of respect. How much of a fight could she put up?

What did the world look like through his eyes?

Aoi's own winrate was just over 2,000. She figured there was still probably a gulf between their ability levels. But based on her experiences analyzing, attempting, and "conquering" everything from schoolwork to basketball to relationships, she thought she might be able to do a little damage. Maybe she could give the famous nanashi a surprise.

*   *   *

In the realm of academics, she'd proved herself in various fights using the methodology she'd cultivated, refining it meticulously.

In the realm of sports, she'd mastered precision moves through repeated trial and error, improving her firepower to the limit.

In the realm of relationships, she'd won repeatedly at mind games by using the tactics she'd developed.

This was her pet theory: Anything with rules and results was a game, life and *Atafami* included.

And she intended to attack nanashi with everything she'd learned in the game of life.

Aoi calmed her pounding heart and pressed the button to confirm.

She knew she wasn't likely to win, but she wasn't about to let him beat her for free, either.

She let out a slow breath and concentrated her attention in the tips of her fingers.

When the game ended, Aoi sat in a daze, the controller still in her hands, staring at the screen.

"…That was amazing."

She'd been no match for him. He crushed her. She hadn't expected to win; she'd assumed a loss was inevitable. But she hadn't expected to completely fail to defend herself at all.

When it came to mastery of fighting techniques, precision of combos, and reads, which she'd considered her specialty—he'd dominated her completely.

"…How'd he do it?"

She had been completely outsmarted, made to dance like a marionette in his palm. He predicted her moves almost as if he were leading her into them, and the instant before she chose a given move, he unleashed the perfect counter.

She had never experienced this before, but it was by no means unpleasant. She was able to realize something as she played—if someone worked really hard at it, they could get this good.

"So that was nanashi…"

She was so excited she almost sent him a chat message—but quickly changed her mind. After all, she was no one in this world. She didn't have the right to talk to him on equal footing yet. Instead of sending a message, she sent a request for another game.

But.

"…Oh."

A second later, nanashi left the room. Yeah, she was insignificant to him at this stage.

"…So that's where I stand."

Nevertheless, she was elated. Memories of the party after the basketball nationals, and of her speech, came flooding back. The loneliness and isolation she'd felt at that moment had left wounds that still ached. Everyone had been saying how fun it was, except for her. For her, winning first place had been a genuine goal, the only thing she wanted. Fun had nothing to do with it. The only things she'd been pursuing were victory, correctness, and something to fill the void. Maybe she really was a monster; maybe understanding and being understood was impossible for her.

But this moment felt completely different.

She thought no one else could put in as much effort as her, or analyze the structure of things so well, or deal with other people so shrewdly. But to him, everything she considered "life" was a speck of dust. To her, that was unimaginable—and that was why her heart felt ready to explode with joy. It was the polar opposite of her experience during her speech after the nationals experience.

This time, she was the one watching the show.

A new sort of hope sprouted in her heart. Maybe the heights she was climbing toward weren't so dark and desolate after all. Maybe someone was waiting up there—someone who had put in even more effort than her.

Yes. Maybe this person had the potential.

Maybe *the champion of the most popular PvP game in Japan* could share this loneliness with her.

She knew nothing.
She looked forward to everything.
Maybe if she took off running toward this goal, she'd be able to reach it this time.
"…Nanashi," she muttered as she turned off the console and opened YouTube on her phone. She was able to find a number of videos of games against him. Whoever posted them probably hadn't gotten his permission, but she didn't care. She added them all to her playlist.
After that, she opened up the Word document she'd been editing. The void within her popped up on-screen—the blank canvas of her *"Midterm Goals."*
Slowly, she typed in a new line of text.

"Be better than nanashi."

She closed the document, and burning with this fierce new determination, she began to analyze nanashi's play style.
I'll start by copying him. It's okay to pretend at first—as long as I eventually start doing everything right.
After all, the real me died on that day, and the real me is no one.

Which means—

If I'm not here anymore, this name means nothing.
I don't need to borrow strength from the sun. I'm strong enough on my own.
Okay—

Giving herself over to this feeling of elation, she opened the settings screen on the console and went to the "name" field. She typed in the characters one at a time, as if she were carving them into her soul. She knew she was empty, but that was exactly the point. She would fill that void with victories she grabbed for herself. She would discard anything she had received from anyone else and prove through her own strength that meaning could be given to a void.

She erased the word *Aoi* and typed in six English letters and one space.

She was intent on covering her first loss. Her movements were imbued with much more passion than when she'd deleted the goal she failed to achieve.

She banged the ENTER key hard with her middle finger, as if she were planting a flag of decision in her life.

At that moment, NO NAME had no idea that a year and a half later, she—as Aoi Hinami—would meet the bottom-tier character nanashi face-to-face.

3

The girlfriend of
the guy I like

Bottom-Tier CHARACTER TOMOZAKI

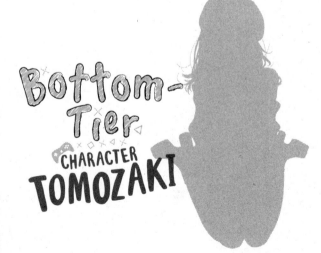

It sucks to say this stuff directly, but it appears that I, Minami Nanami, have been rejected in love.

I have this bad habit of distancing myself from my emotions when I've been hurt. It seems like it should make me feel a little better, but the truth is, it doesn't really work. The problem is that I can't stop trying to escape reality anyway.

I want someone to praise me, to tell me I did a wonderful thing and everything will be all right, because after all, I did push the guy I like toward another girl. I'm not trying to say that anything would be different for me right now if I hadn't done that, but they're dating now thanks to me. I think that counts as a successful assist—like when the ref blows the whistle just as the other player makes a three-pointer. Go, Minami! Except the ball went into my own basket.

I'm an expert on myself, which means I know more about myself than anyone else does—at least, I think I do, but I'm always tripping over my own feet. It's been a problem for a long time. Basically, what happens is that I think I should do one thing, but then I get in trouble and give up what I wanted to somebody else. So like, fine, whatever—at least they got something good out of it, right? But a part of me doesn't really think that. I've done the same thing millions of times, which makes me wonder—what do I want anyway?

When I start thinking I'm the only one who ever loses out, that's a sign that I'm really starting to spiral into regret. All these little scrapes and scratches feel like they're bleeding tears more than blood—and fun fact! Tears and blood are made of almost identical components. I try to brush things over with fun little facts like that, but who am I even trying to fool right now?

I do know one thing, though. First, my head is probably going to feel fuzzy for this whole winter break. And second, this time I definitely lost the thing I wanted. I know, I know—that was two things, not one, but let's not get hung up on the details. To me, the two things are basically one anyway.

So what did I decide to do? Same thing I've always done. Go on living my life cheerfully, happily, and noisily.

* * *

It was a coincidence, but I'd be lying if I said I didn't have a small hunch that it might happen. After all, it's the kind of place you'd expect to find her.

"Oh...Nanami-san and Natsubayashi-san...?"

A few days had passed since the school festival party, and we were getting close to New Year's Day. Tama and I had been walking around snow-covered Omiya when we came to a stylish café, and it happened. Tama was sitting across from me at a table when who else but Fuka-chan should appear.

"Fuka-chan?"

Incredibly, she was wearing a maid costume and carrying a tray with glasses of water in one hand. For a second, she looked so perfect I thought she was a snow sprite, but since we were inside, I decided that couldn't be. Which meant she must work here. I stared at her as she stood there blushing uneasily.

"What are you wearing?! It's so adorable!"

She had on glasses, which she doesn't usually wear, and a maid costume that was a little tamer than the cosplay ones but still supercute on her. The second I saw her I was just about knocked out.

"That looks so perfect on you! I wish you'd wear that to school!"

"Uh, um..."

"Can I take a picture?! Please! I won't show it to anyone else."

"Um, well..."

"Minmi. You're putting Kikuchi-san on the spot," Tama snapped, obviously displeased that I was bothering Fuka-chan. Then all of a sudden, she started giggling and shook her head. I love the way her expression changes from second to second, and she even had another adorable creature standing right next to her. It was a double whammy. I wouldn't be surprised if they charged me extra for this harem experience.

"I'm sorry about Minmi. So you've got a part-time job here?"

"Y-yes."

While I was incapable of not being a weirdo, Tama was being super nice to Kikuchi-san. Ever since the thing with Erika, Tama's been so kind, and she's gotten so good at interacting with people. She doesn't even need me anymore. I'm happy she's matured so much, but she's still adorable, so I fully intend to continue hitting on her.

"This café is so perfect for you," Tama said, looking around.

"R-really...? Thanks so much."

"Um, how long have you worked here?"

"Since the start of second year..."

"Wow!"

I stood by chewing on my finger while the two of them had this nice conversation. I wondered why Tama was acting a little more proactive than usual, but I was getting to watch a lovely exchange between these two for free, so why worry? And I'm an honest woman, so when I say I was chewing on my finger, I mean I was literally chewing on my finger.

"Well...I'll come back when you're ready to order."

"Sounds good!"

"What? You're leaving? I'll be so lonely! Come back soon!"

"Um, okay."

I wiggled with excitement at the confused look she gave me, waving good-bye as she set the water on our table and left. She returned my wave sedately, which just made the wiggles worse. So cute!

"This really is a great place."

"We haven't even tried the food yet."

"Oh right."

I was still excited about our unexpected encounter, but Tama was as cool as always. Maybe the reason she's able to stay so calm in the presence of such an adorable creature is because she's an adorable creature herself.

"It really does suit her…," I couldn't help muttering. I mean, Fuka-chan really is cute. She's so graceful you'd think she was some sort of aristocrat, and she has this naturally good smell, too. Not like perfume; more like soap or shampoo or something. Her hair is silky, but it's her face that's so pretty. She's got all the elements of a perfect teenage girl, *and* she's wearing a maid costume? You could knock me over with a feather.

"Yeah, well, why don't you get yourself one?" Tama asked.

I imagined myself wearing a maid costume, but I'm not sure I'd look so great. Maybe it wouldn't be horrible on me, but I'd definitely look like I was doing cosplay. I mean, I don't have that fairy aura that Fuka-chan has, and it's pretty hard to imagine a noisy, rowdy maid.

"Nope, I don't think I'm the type for it," I said honestly.

Fuka-chan is all airy and fluffy, with that waifish figure and pale skin, but at the same time, I feel like she's got a spine. You could imagine her as the heroine of some story. She's totally different from me. I'm always loud.

As I was thinking all this, I suddenly sensed something murky rising up from the depths of my heart. I mean, guys prefer that kind of—

"…Minmi?"

Snapping back to reality, I realized that Tama was peering into my face. Damn, that was close. I might have become Dark Mimimi again. Lately, Dark Mimimi has been poking her nasty head out the second I let down my guard, so I really have to pay attention all the time.

Jealousy and self-loathing pile up like snow in my heart; even if I try to shovel it out of the way, it ends up sticking around in some corner. I know I've just got to wait for it to melt, but in the meantime, I have to be careful not to slip and fall on it.

"…What? What's up, Tama?" I smiled, pretending everything was fine. Smiling like that is my secret weapon. Even sharp little Tama usually can't see through it to what I'm really feeling.

"…Oh, nothing."

She seemed slightly dissatisfied, but she was nice enough to drop it.

Even if she notices something is off, she won't ask if I don't say anything. Tama's good with boundaries. I respect that about her.

"You know, you can always talk to me," she commented. Somehow, the words were brusque and brimming with affection at the same time. I think it's her way of showing her love.

"I know. Thanks."

I considered telling her what was on my mind but decided not to. Tama knows I'm close with Tomozaki, but she doesn't know I told him my feelings. It's not that I'm keeping it secret. It's just that I don't want to show her more of my weaknesses and lean on her too much.

Plus—if I said something now, when Tomozaki's already dating Fuka-chan, she probably wouldn't know what to say.

"Anyway, what should we order?! Everything looks so good! I'm starving!"

As I always did, I waved it all away in my usual loud, cheerful way and examined the menu, which had a sort of trendy fantasy vibe. Tama nodded and started studying the options with me. I did feel like I was hiding something from her—but only partly. I mean, I really was starving.

* * *

After we finished eating, we hung out and relaxed at the café. The hamburger I ordered was super delicious, and my only regret was that the lunch rush meant I didn't have a chance to hit on Fuka-chan again. I was feeling calmer by then, so I figured I'd better make up for lost time.

"Even the tea is amazing!" I said, elegantly sipping my after-lunch cup of black tea.

Usually, I load it up with milk and sugar, but this café probably had some kind of special blend. I decided to skip the milk and go light on the sugar, which turned out to be an excellent decision. The faint sweetness and rich aroma made for the perfect cuppa. Hee-hee, I sound like a grown-up, right?

"I know, it's delicious!" said Tama, who'd ordered the lemon tea.

"The hamburgers here are excellent, and Fuka-chan is cute. I think we've found the ideal café..."

"Just don't harass the staff, okay?"

Tama-chan never fails to see through to my ulterior motives. It would've been cute if she was saying that because she didn't want me to hit on anyone except her, but there was something exciting about the way she ignored me, too.

We chatted aimlessly for a few more minutes, then suddenly Tama stood up.

"I'm going to the restroom."

"Okay. Want me to come with?"

"No, it's fine."

With that, she marched off toward the bathroom. She looked so cute from behind, I considered tackling her, but we weren't in school right now. I know these things have a time and a place.

Sitting there by myself was kinda boring, and I started scanning the room for Fuka-chan so I could figure out a way to bug her again, when...

"It was nice to see you today!"

...I heard a crystal-clear voice coming from the entrance and turned in that direction. Who should I see but Fuka-chan, wearing her street clothes and saying good-bye to the other café staff. Yes! This was going to be a piece of cake.

I waved cheerfully at her. "Fuka-chan!"

She looked over and smiled nervously, then slowly walked in my direction. The perfect chance to do a little flirting!

"Is your shift over?"

"Y-yes, it is."

I glanced at my phone. It was after three. She'd probably been working since morning and just finished. Perfect.

"Well, then, my dear, would you like to join us for a cup of tea?"

My cute-girl radar was blaring so loud, I accidentally went for an old-fashioned pickup line. She seems like the hard-to-get type, so I thought she'd say no.

I really did.

But after pausing for a moment, she said, "Um, well...I'd love to."

There was so much determination behind her expression. Well, this was an unexpected twist. Wasn't she nervous to talk to me without Tama there? For once, I felt a little nervous myself.

"Uh, no pressure. You can say no if you don't want to," I said as nicely as possible.

"Um…it's fine. I do want to."

"…Really?"

So she said, but she was obviously nervous, and even though I was the one who invited her, I didn't know why she would go so far outside her comfort zone to accept my invitation. On the other hand, we'd hardly ever talked before, so it could be a good opportunity—

But as I thought about it, my excitement began to cool. I'd called out to her on the spur of the moment, but was this going to be awkward? I mean, Fuka-chan was dating the guy I'd asked out myself. The whirling thoughts in my head were stirring up anxiety.

Does Fuka-chan know what I told Tomozaki?
If she knows, what does she think about it?
If she doesn't, should I tell her?
If I tell her…do I have to stop talking to Tomozaki?

As I was mulling over these questions, a woman in her twenties, who must have been Fuka-chan's manager, noticed us and came over.

"Oh, Kikuchi-san, is this your friend? I'll bring over some cake for everyone, no charge!" she offered cheerfully. Now there was no going back.

"Oh, thank you so much," I said.

"Umm…" Fuka-chan looked back and forth between her manager and me, smiling uncomfortably. "Okay, do you mind if I sit here?" She sat down across from me and nervously straightened her back.

"Of course not! Welcome!"

Somehow, her nervousness was spreading to me. Our one-on-one dialogue had begun.

* * *

"Um…"

Fuka-chan's eyes were darting around anxiously, which made her look even more like a little squirrel or something. I think she was searching for a topic. *Fear not, Mimimi-chan will handle that!*

"So! I never expected you and the Brain to start dating!"

Yeah, I was barging straight into the main topic, but this wasn't the time to beat around the bush—and I'll admit, if she did know something, I wanted to lure her into saying it herself. I know, I'm sneaky.

"So you think it's unexpected?" she said, glancing at me questioningly. Given the topic, I was feeling anxious, too, but I made an effort to act normal.

"No, maybe not. What I mean is…Tomozaki doesn't seem to have the same interests as you."

Fuka-chan giggled happily. "You could be right. I bet he doesn't pay attention to anything he doesn't like."

"Exactly!" I said, smiling. "He said it's 'cause he's a gamer, but I still think he's kind of extreme!"

"Tee-hee. I know."

"Right?"

We were really getting into this conversation about Tomozaki. *Hey, wait a second, are we warming up to each other?* I was also thinking that she didn't seem to know about me and Tomozaki, which I admit may have been slightly sneaky of me. But also, watching her get so happy talking about Tomozaki did prick my heart a little. I don't like that part of myself, but I can't hold back Dark Mimimi when she starts to think like that.

"I have a hard time imagining what the two of you talk about," I said, slyly nudging the conversation toward uncovering more about the two of them.

"What we talk about?" she said, thinking for a moment. "We've talked about the future, the best way to live…"

"Wow, that's so deep!" I blurted out. Those were lofty topics—but they did seem like things Tomozaki would talk about. Was that what I was missing in his eyes? My chest tightened. On the other hand, it was kind of messed up for me to go out of my way to ask something like that and then get hurt by the answer.

"Um, has he said anything about me? I won't let him get away with gossiping about me!"

I almost asked her straight out what was on my mind. I wanted to know. The truth was, I wanted to know something a lot more important than gossip, but I couldn't help being a little silly to cover up the seriousness of it. One day the gods will punish me for acting like this.

"Talked about you...?"

"Yes."

"Um..."

She thought for a moment, while I quivered in fear of this totally trivial thing. If she did know everything, then she might have known exactly what I was up to. Several tension-filled seconds passed. Finally, she awkwardly said, "Not really... He just said you walk home from the station together and you're friends..."

"Oh, really?"

She didn't seem to be hiding anything. I was pretty sure she didn't know. But at the same time, it was sort of depressing that the Brain hadn't talked about me. Knowing him, he probably thought it would be wrong to say anything to her, but... *Come on, Brain, was that all my confession of love meant to you?! Wait, what am I saying?!*

When I calmed down enough to think, I realized it was wrong to poke around the edges like this. Putting a nice person like Fuka-chan on the spot really wasn't the right thing to do.

"Actually...," I said, deciding to atone for my sin by confessing. "A little while ago...I told the Brain...that I liked him."

"What?!" she said in a louder voice than I've ever heard her use before, her eyes going all round.

"Sorry that was so sudden!"

"Oh, no, um..."

Her eyes darted around like she didn't know what to say. Well, yeah. She was sitting across from a potential rival, and now she was dating the

guy in question. Of course she didn't know what to say. They were dating already, end of story. She couldn't exactly say, *Sorry I stole him,* but she wasn't mean enough to act totally unfazed. It really put her in a tight spot.

"No, I'm the one who lost!"

All I could do at that point was be as loud and cheerful as possible.

"L-lost...?"

"Yeah! I liked the Brain, too, right? But he chose you. It was a battle of hearts! No hard feelings!"

"Er, battle...?"

"Yes! But don't worry about it...although I know that's easier said than done. I just wanted to do the right thing!" I said in my usual cheery way, giving her a thumbs-up in hopes of easing the tension.

She gazed at me solemnly. Her expression was still a little frightened, but her voice was completely calm as she finally spoke.

"Um...I don't think it's a battle."

"Really? You don't?"

I'd used that word without much thought, but I couldn't help flinching at her serious reaction. I know I've got a bad habit of talking without thinking, but I don't want people to see what's really going on in my heart. Trying to hide is just instinct. Actually, I felt like I'd been spinning my wheels for a while in this conversation.

"I think there are many reasons two people end up in a romantic relationship..."

"...Uh-huh?"

The way she said it was kind of awkward, but I think it was just because she was doing her best to treat me seriously. Which meant that even a sneaky girl like me had to make an attempt to be earnest.

"For example, they have similar goals, or they simply enjoy spending time together...or they complement each other's weak spots...I think those are some of the reasons."

I could see her point.

"I think I get what you're saying. When I like someone, it usually falls into one of those categories."

"Tee-hee. Me too." She smiled mischievously.

"Wait, so you're saying you've had crushes on lots of people in the past?"

"Of course! I'm a girl, too, you know."

"Wow, that's a surprise!"

We shared a smile, and I felt a little closer to her. Romantic gossip really was a great way for girls to become friends. Although I kinda wish it hadn't started with my underhanded question.

"What you said about complementing each other's weak spots is interesting," I said, sensing that needle pricking my heart again. "...It probably doesn't work when the complementing only goes one way, huh?"

Fuka-chan peered at me with her beautiful, clear eyes. Then she said slowly, "Is that what happened with you?"

I felt like she'd just seen straight into my heart with that quiet, overwhelming power of hers. I like to think I'm good at conversation, but in that moment, I suddenly had no idea what to say. But I didn't feel like she'd invaded my privacy—more like she was simply peering deep inside of me.

Did I just want someone to make up for what I was missing without being able to offer anything in return? The question was fairly painful for me to consider.

"Um, well..."

"Oh, sorry, that was a rude question!"

"No, not at all!"

I was surprised to suddenly be confronted with a question that reached my core, but it wasn't rude. She was just being straightforward—I was the one at fault for beating around the bush.

Plus, if I was going to bring up a topic like this and try to trick her into revealing information, then maybe I owed it to her to admit a few of my own secrets.

"I think...," I began.

"Yes?" she said, listening attentively.

"I think I envied Tomozaki for having such a strong core."

"Mm...," she said, nodding before settling in to listen again.

"And the reason I fell for him…was because when we were together, he made up for something I didn't have, y'know?" I said lightly.

Fuka-chan seemed to be thinking seriously about what I'd said. "Do you mean that when you were together, you felt a little bit stronger?"

"Hmm, maybe."

"And…you liked yourself more when you were with him?"

"That might be it!"

She really nailed it. When I'm with him, his strength spreads to me, and that's why I feel so at ease. Normally, I don't like myself that much, but when I'm with him, I do.

"Tee-hee. I know how you feel. Tomozaki is timid, but he's got that strength."

I had to laugh. She got it.

"Ah-ha-ha. I know exactly what you mean." And yet breathing was getting harder and harder.

"Once he makes up his mind to do something, he won't give up until he's done it."

"…Yeah."

Weak but strong.

"He won't change direction just because somebody tells him to."

Cowardly but sure of his path.

"He believes in himself."

The thought that occurred to me right then is probably a sign that I'm a bad person. But there's no way I can brush over that cold, small feeling. I mean, I *did* think it.

I wanted to be the only one who knew how cool Tomozaki could be.

As the person he rejected, I know I shouldn't be thinking that. He chose Fuka-chan, so naturally she would know at least that much about him. Still, that girl inside of me was screaming.

"I…really like those things about him, too."

"Ah-ha-ha… I bet. Makes sense."

The more she talked, the worse I felt. I wanted to jam my fingers into my ears. But I still couldn't bring myself to dislike her. I agreed completely with every word she was saying.

I could never hate someone who had so many good things to say about the guy I like.

"...Yup."

At the same time, I realized something. The fact that I felt this way meant that—

"I think I still like him."

"...Hmm."

I decided to tell her the truth. "I haven't given up on him yet."

"Yes...that's what I thought."

She looked straight at me, and I couldn't tell what she was thinking. I didn't detect any hostility or anger in her eyes.

"I don't plan to do anything bad, but I'm going to be true to myself." My words sounded more like an athlete's oath than a declaration of war. "Is that okay?" I was surprised by how calm I felt after that.

"I don't think there can be any wrong answers when it comes to liking someone."

"Wrong answers?"

That was an odd thing to say. She nodded and continued, like she was confronting me head-on with her beliefs.

"Some people fall for strong people they look up to, and others fall for weak people they think they can save. Some people like being pursued, and some people's feelings grow stronger out of jealousy."

"Yeah...I guess you're right."

Her words swept over me, as quiet as the woods. I nodded slowly, but I still didn't know what she was getting at. I watched her intently as she went on.

"Whatever the reason...," she said, pausing to search for the right words. "If you like someone, it's not wrong."

For some reason, she was clearly trying very hard to convince me.

"That's why...I want to respect your feelings for Tomozaki."

Now that she'd said that, there was no way I could dislike her.

"...You do? Thank you," I said, genuinely grateful. I never expected Tomozaki's girlfriend to affirm my feelings for him. After a few seconds, she seemed to realize something and frantically added, "Oh, I'm sorry... Maybe it's not my place to say something like that..."

"Ah-ha-ha. Good point."

"Right...!"

She was so cute when she got flustered. I couldn't hate her. If anything, I was developing a crush on her myself.

"Thank you. I mean it."

* * *

By then, Tama was heading back to the table, so we stopped talking about Tomozaki. Instead, we hung out for an hour or so talking about the play and entrance exams and stuff before we got ready to leave.

"Well...I'm going to stop at the bookstore, so I'd better be going."

"Gotcha! Thanks, Fuka-chan—that was fun!"

"Take care!"

As Tama and I saw her off, she waved at us with a smile.

"I had a good time, too! Well, um, bye!"

"Bye!"

"See you later!"

Even as I waved cheerfully, I was swooning inside. Hearing the one and only Fuka-chan say she had a good time was almost too much for me.

"That was an odd little get-together," I commented to Tama as I watched Fuka-chan walk across the street from the train station.

Tama ignored me at first, but as I turned toward the station, she hit me with a fastball.

"You had feelings for Tomozaki, right?"

"What?!" I yelped, looking behind me reflexively. I got into the weeds with Fuka-chan, too, so I guess it was just that kind of day?

"Wh-wh-wh-why'd you say that?!"

"It's obvious," she replied. Apparently, I wasn't going to be able to sweep this under the rug.

"Um, well...I did l-like him, but..."

"I knew it."

She sighed. It's like she has the mind of an adult in the body of a child.

"Did everything go okay with you and Kikuchi-san?"

I was thrown off again by her totally straightforward question, but I could sense how kind she'd gotten compared to before. Interesting. She decided to bring this up because she saw me and Fuka-chan talking.

"You were worried about me?" I asked.

"Of course I was. When I came out of the bathroom and was about to head back to the table, you two seemed to be in some sort of complicated conversation."

"Oh...hey, wait," I said, catching on to something. That must mean... "Did you kill time until we were done?"

She pouted. "Obviously. I wouldn't interrupt a conversation like that. I can read the room."

"Ah-ha-ha, never thought I'd hear *you* talking about reading the room."

"I can pay attention when I want to!"

"Hmm..."

That made me happy, but I was also remembering my talk with Fuka-chan. Basically, we'd shared our true feelings and understood each other a little better.

"It was fine. We just talked about our feelings. No arguments or anything."

"Really?"

"Really." I nodded, but something was still bothering me. "...Tama, do you think the reason I liked the Brain...was because I wanted to lean on his strength?"

"That was a sudden question!"

"Kikuchi-san and I were talking about it—about why I had a crush on him."

"Huh," she said softly, giving me an appraising look. "Do you think that was the only reason?"

"Yes."

"Why?"

Her surprisingly direct question was reassuring in a sense, but I didn't have a ready answer. Why *did* I like him? I think my answer was different from Fuka-chan's. I looked Tama-chan in the eye, as if we were analyzing me together.

"...It's tough getting through everything on my own, but changing is even harder, so I think I just relied on someone stronger than me."

Whoops, that was really serious. But Tama just listened with the same expression on her face.

"But if I was just relying on him, did I really like him? Should I have even told him? Fuka-chan said it was okay, but I'm not sure."

I feel like Fuka-chan's way of thinking is similar to Tomozaki's, and their general personality is kind of similar, too. They probably started dating for a lot of different reasons. By comparison, I'd started to think that I just saw him as someone who could carry my emotional baggage.

Tama listened thoughtfully to my sudden revelation.

"Well, this is just my opinion, but..."

"Yeah?"

"I agree that it's not always easy to be the one people rely on. It's a heavy thing on your shoulders."

"That sounds bad."

Her words cut straight into my heart.

"I'm not done," she said, smiling in a way that felt like a hug.

"I also think being leaned on can be a very warm feeling."

She tapped my chest.

"So I don't think you should worry about it too much."

It was like a weight was instantly lifted from my heart.

"Ah-ha-ha. Thanks. I really owe you one."

"You're welcome."

As usual lately, she met my serious words of gratitude with a silly smug look. I love her for that. I actually think I might have a crush on Tama *and* Fuka-chan *and* Tomozaki—so in a sense, I'm a really lucky girl.

"Ah, life, so full of twists and turns."

Tama and I kept walking along beneath the cold sky. Snow was still piled deep along the edges of the streets in Omiya, but the warm sunshine was gradually beginning to melt it.

4 Lies and morning glow

Bottom-Tier
CHARACTER
TOMOZAKI

They were in an apartment in the Meguro district.

Startled awake by a sudden sensation against his calf, the man opened his eyes. Rena was lying with her back to him, looking at her phone. He wrapped his arm around her shoulder.

"Morning, Rena," he whispered into her ear, lightly hugging her from behind. He could feel her supple skin through the thin fabric of her Gelato Pique loungewear. Her hair smelled faintly of sweat.

"Hmm?" she said in a cutesy voice, then closed the Twitter app she'd been looking at. Accepting his embrace, she turned her head and gave him a vulnerable smile.

"…Morning. Did I wake you up?"

"Yeah. I don't mind."

"You don't?"

She wiggled her hips and flipped over so she was facing him. Then she reached her arms up and laced her fingers behind his neck. Squeezed between her arms, her cleavage deepened and brushed the man's body ever so slightly. She gazed up at him coyly.

"…I was thinking…"

"What?" he asked, revealing his interest as her sultry eyes focused on him.

"I think you know," she said. She wasn't hiding her excitement.

"What are you talking about?" he said, feigning ignorance. She nuzzled closer to him. Their bodies pressed together, and he could feel her warmth and softness. Her lips brushed his ear, her breathy voice tickling his eardrums.

*   *   *

"Let's do it again."

Like a spark fanning into a flame, he pulled her to him, just a little more roughly this time.

* * *

Five or six hours earlier, Rena had been in a free space in Shibuya. The year was almost over, and Tokyo was still blanketed in snow. Twelve men and three women were gathered in the simple, white room furnished only with tables, chairs, and a cooking area. They were there for a real-world meetup for players of a well-known FPS game.

It was after ten at night. They'd been there for about two hours, and by this time, everyone was moving around talking to whoever they wanted. Rena looked around in a haze, her thinking blurred from drinking.

"You know the video I put up the other day...?"

"I'll follow you on Twitter..."

As the excited voices ricocheted inside her head, she felt like she was melting airily into the crowd. The shoulders peeking out from the cutouts in her oversized black sweater were flushed pink. It was obvious that she was drunk, but she didn't mind.

"You been drinking, Rena-chan?"

A man had sat down next to her, set his chin comfortably in his hand, and started talking; he went by the name Rambo. That was his gaming handle; Rena didn't know his real name. He looked like your typical office worker, probably in his early thirties. He said he edited online videos. Behind him, Rena saw he'd brought a younger coworker named Old Man Hippo. Needless to say, this was also a gaming handle.

"Yes, I have. Haven't you?" she replied playfully to Rambo, who was probably a decade older than her. They'd met for the first time that evening and hadn't talked much yet, but Rena was already addressing him like a friend.

Old Man Hippo watched them from a few steps back.

"Me? Yeah, I'm drinking," Rambo said, going along with her friendly tone. He seemed to enjoy it, which was good because it could have been taken as rude.

Rena was almost elated that it had gone over so well.

"Really?"

"Really."

Yes, she'd won him over. There was a certain type of man who couldn't resist her catlike friendliness, who instantly started fawning expectantly over her. She knew that from experience.

"I see your glass is empty. Shall I get you something?" he asked in a vaguely theatrical tone.

"Yes, what are you going to have?" Old Man Hippo said, jumping in as if he'd finally found a role for himself in the conversation.

Rena smirked a little at his pointless contribution.

"Hmm, let's see...," she said, as if she were carefully weighing their words.

Rambo was watching her carefully. But when she met his gaze, he quickly glanced away, as if he couldn't handle it. From there, his glance flickered to her chest, outlined clearly by the sweater dress, to her legs below the short hem, before settling eventually on a wall or his phone. As if she wouldn't notice.

Old Man Hippo was even worse. He was staring unswervingly at Rambo, like he was trying to avoid Rena, and hadn't made eye contact with her once. Then, when he thought she wasn't looking, his eyes would dart over to her. Rena sighed softly to herself, holding off on answering their question.

This type again...

"...How about I make you a mixed drink?" Rambo asked, apparently unable to stand the silence. The flirtatious way he said it—"How about I make you one?" not "How about we go get something together?"—brought her out of her drunken haze. She looked at Rambo with his insincere, uptight expression and at Old Man Hippo, who was still shooting furtive glances at her, and pasted a happy smile on her face.

"That's okay; I'll go get something myself. Wait for me, 'kay?"

"Are you sure...?"

"Of course!"

What boring men.

Having written them off, she stood up and walked over to the counter. Her flushed shoulders were bare, while her sweater hid little of her long legs, and her nude stockings made them look bare. She glanced back at the two men. Both of them were staring after her greedily.

I'm the object of their desire.

The thought excited her, and she felt a warm, satisfied sensation spreading over her lower abdomen.

They want me. But they can't have me.

As she walked, she tilted her empty glass up to her lips, drinking down the melted ice. The clear liquid chilled her mouth, but her chest remained warm. She'd told them to wait for her—but she had no intention of returning.

* * *

Every time Rena came to a meetup like this, multiple guys approached her. She had regular features that she highlighted with makeup and a feminine figure that she accentuated with suggestive clothes and shoes. All of it was selected with men's desires in mind. She was slightly annoyed when the guys who hit on her weren't her type, but the excitement of being desired far outweighed the irritation. Whenever they expressed their interest, she inevitably remembered a cardinal truth: Women always lie, and men are always honest.

"We get along so well, Rena. I can really be myself around you."

"Stay away from me, you traitor."

"I knew it! I knew we'd get along great!"

"Can you believe she told me I shouldn't worry about it? That's not how real friends act."

"!"

She leaned on the kitchen window and propped her chin on her palm, scowling. Outside, the snow was beginning to melt on the streets of Shibuya. Pushed to the edges of the sidewalk and crushed underfoot into a slushy mess, it reminded her of a person who had revealed their true self.

She gazed out at it, her mind wandering. The haze of alcohol had brought forward a memory from three years earlier that she couldn't care less about.

She had been seventeen then, still in high school.

She'd already nearly perfected her style, and her classmates—especially the guys—admired her looks. They didn't want to date her, really—just to mess around with her. She was casually aware of that fact. Wearing her uniform skirt short was an intentional choice, but the way her gym clothes drew attention to her wasn't. She was a typical high school girl in that she found her feminine body annoying at times, at least back then.

She belonged to the most popular group, probably because her looks drew people to her. It wasn't that everyone in the group got along—more like they used one another as accessories to strengthen their own position in the hierarchy. They had an interest in one another, you might say.

"Ooh, did you redo your nails, Rena?"

"You noticed! Sharp eyes, Shoko! I thought I'd try something a little bolder."

"The black and pink looks so cute together. It really suits you."

"Really? Thank you!"

Every time she talked with someone else in the popular group, they evaluated one another's aesthetic, like they were keeping a watch on each other. She updated her look competitively. Sometimes, they competed with each other, and at other times, they formed a faction to gain the upper hand over another group. In a sense, they were just passing time together.

"Rena, you don't keep anything secret from me, do you?"

"Why are you asking me that? Of course I never lie."

"I can trust you that way. I feel like we really get along."

"You do?"

Setting aside the question of how deep the other girl's trust really was, Rena would have been lying if she claimed the approval didn't make her happy.

If anything set her aside from the others, it was her tendency to really get into her hobbies. Aside from belonging to the popular group, she also belonged to a group of girls with various obsessions. One was really into visual kei bands, another was a fan of certain online gamers who streamed with face cams, and another followed underground boy bands. Then there was Rena, who liked online gaming. A handful of these girls, all of whom were attractive and flashy but had somehow strayed from the norm, had crossed the boundaries between class cliques to form their own small core group.

Rena didn't feel that she was more her real self in one group versus the other. If she had to put it into words, she might have said that she needed both groups in order to fit both sides of herself—the side that was pretty and the side that easily became obsessed with hobbies—into the school community. However, her unique position ended up getting her into some minor trouble.

One day, Rena was walking home after school with her classmate Karen, a member of the core group. She often watched videos on the streaming site TwitCasting and was a fan of several streamers.

"So does that day work for you?" Karen asked her. "I was thinking we could do it at my house."

"Yeah, that's good for me," Rena answered.

They were talking about a video game that several members of their group liked. It was an FPS game you could play on a phone either online or locally, and they were planning a get-together to play.

"Awesome. So it'll be you, me, Kaoru, Chiri, and..."

"Wait, you invited other people?"

Karen had already named the four core members of their group, and Rena had assumed that would be it.

"Yeah...Keisuke-kun, Makoto-kun, Yosuke-kun, and 'Yamaken'-san from the grade ahead of us."

"Wow, nice! How'd you get them to say yes?"

"Apparently, they're really into this game."

"Cool."

All four boys had gone to the same school as Rena and Karen but now were in university or working. They'd all been very popular, and lots of the younger kids had envied them. Rena hadn't been especially close with any of them, but their names alone were enough to make her excited.

A private party with the four of them. And on top of that, they'd be playing the game Rena loved. She was at a stage in life where that idea was enough to unleash happy butterflies in her chest.

"Okay, so I'll leave that day open," she said in a laid-back tone. She was looking forward to it.

On the day of the party, she went to Karen's house. But the scene that unfolded in Karen's room wasn't quite what she had imagined.

A mixed group of eight was in the small room. They'd played a few games at the beginning, but after that, it had devolved into a kind of singles party. Some of the girls and guys had their arms around each other's waists or shoulders. You'd never have guessed they were meeting for the first time that day.

"Come over here, Rena-chan."

"What do you want, Yosuke-kun? Oh well, I guess it's fine."

The situation had gone a bit beyond what she expected, but for some reason, she felt comfortable there. Of course, common sense told her this wasn't pure, innocent fun, and she knew the boys didn't really respect her. But she felt like she'd been let in early to the adult world. That feeling of superiority made her let her guard down.

But a few days later, a problem came up.

"Hey, Rena, I heard you went to Karen's party."

"What, you mean with Keisuke and those guys?"

"Yeah."

She was in the classroom after school when Shoko, a member of the popular group, approached her sullenly.

"Yosuke-kun was there, too, right?"

"Yeah."

Shoko frowned. "You knew I was dating him, didn't you?"

"Yes, but…I thought you broke up."

She still didn't understand what Shoko was after.

"That's not the issue."

"…What's the issue?" Rena asked.

Shoko looked obviously angry now. "It hasn't even been two weeks since we split up. Don't you think it's a little insensitive to go after someone's ex that fast?"

"…Is it?" she asked. She didn't see the problem.

Yosuke *was* Shoko's ex, and he *had* put his arm around Rena's shoulder and gotten kind of friendly with her. But what was wrong with that? She genuinely thought it was fine, but maybe she'd been feeling even more casual about it because she'd been part of such a grown-up party. If anything, it was immature of Shoko to get hung up about something so minor.

"If you're not together anymore, I don't think it matters how long it's been."

"Are you serious?"

"Yes."

"Fine. I don't know what else to say," Shoko said, then spun on her heels and walked off.

"Such a baby," Rena said, loud enough for Shoko to hear, and Shoko shot her a nasty look.

Starting the next day, Shoko *and* her friends acted differently toward Rena.

"Morning."

"Umm…"

In the morning, when Rena tried to say hello to another member of the popular group, the other girl acted uncomfortable, like she didn't know what to say. Rena didn't know exactly what was going on, but she was a free spirit. Figuring the girl must be sleepy or something, she turned to another girl without making a big deal of it. The problem was, everyone acted the same way. Whoever she tried to talk to in the popular group, they looked awkwardly away from her. By the time Shoko and every other member had reacted the same way, Rena understood fully.

She had been ostracized.

They had never been super close friends anyway. In this group, whose members used one another like accessories, even the faintest crack could easily break the cohesion. Still, Rena remembered what Shoko had once said to her. *"We get along so well. I can really be myself around you."* Those words had made Rena happy, and in a way, she'd felt she'd found her place.

"Ugh."

For a little while at least, she would be isolated in her class. She laughed at the ridiculousness of it.

"...It really is childish," she snapped, but no one was listening.

After that, Rena was constantly alone at school. She'd always been strong-willed and upfront about her likes and dislikes, so being rejected by Shoko and her group was enough to make her lose her place in the school overall. What she hadn't expected was that the members of her core group would gradually begin to avoid her as well. But their interests had never been entirely aligned anyway. Visual kei bands, underground rock, streamers, online gaming—they'd come together to ease their isolation, because no one else accepted their obsessions. They attracted attention, but they didn't have a strong position. They didn't have the leeway to retain a member who had been rejected by the popular group. Meaning that single incident caused Rena to lose both groups she'd felt at home in.

Of course, Shoko probably hadn't intended to keep shunning Rena until they graduated. She'd only meant to make an example of her because Rena had hit her where she was weakest. They should have found a chance to make up after a few weeks.

But a few days after Rena became an outcast, she began to skip class and soon stopped attending class altogether. The isolation itself hadn't gotten to her exactly, but being alienated at school was much more unpleasant than she'd expected. When she was in the popular group, classmates had moved aside obsequiously when she passed. Now those girls who Rena saw as plain and unattractive frowned and avoided her if she came near. They talked about her loud enough for her to overhear.

"Ugh, she's coming over here."

"I sure am," she would say back, refusing to give in to them. But at school, unless you had multiple people on your side, turning the tide wasn't possible.

"It's her fault for coming."

"I wish she wouldn't."

"Same here."

"..."

She could defend herself all she wanted, but she may as well have said nothing. And she was cuter than them, and her figure was better! She was far ahead of them.

She frowned and pouted, but no one came to her side. Now that she didn't belong to any group, she was suddenly dropped to the rock bottom of the hierarchy. Anybody watching would have felt sorry for her. She decided she'd be better off disappearing altogether before she started feeling it, too.

Once she wasn't at school, the hierarchy was gone. She had no reason to meet with her classmates or group members, so they could no longer force their lies on her with the violence of numbers. Instead, she began to meet regularly with the guys who had been at Karen's party.

"Sorry I'm late, Rena-chan."

"Should we go?"

Keisuke, Makoto, Yosuke, and Yamaken. Before long, she was close with several of them, including Shoko's ex, Yosuke. Eventually, she started dating Keisuke, their leader.

"Rena, I heard you quit school."

"Yeah, I did."

"Huh… Well, you'll figure something out. You're hot."

"Ah-ha-ha," she laughed, slipping her arm through Keisuke's. "…Yes, I think I will."

She didn't feel guilty at that moment, much less pitiful. No—she felt superior. She'd lost her place at school, but she was second to no one. All these cool university guys wanted her. She had multiple strongholds. These guys had been popular since high school, idols of the younger students. They were far more valuable to her than some random rules that changed with the whims of the majority, far more valuable than friendships that only went skin deep.

At school, her place among the girls had been stolen from her. Mood and words were everything in that realm, and she'd been dragged through the dirt. But instincts didn't lie. Guys were forced to show their true colors when she confronted them with her womanliness. That's why she didn't believe in words—she believed in feelings. Not logic, only instinct.

Chin in hand, Rena gazed at the dirty snow outside the window. It was gray and slushy with footprints, but if you cut away the top layer, fresh white snow appeared again. Liars were the same way—the first time they met a guy, they showed that innocent, unspoiled side. Rena stood in front of the kitchen counter, looking around the meetup. How many of these people were really innocent? As for herself, she at least wanted to be like honest, dirty snow from the start.

What a stupid memory. The alcohol had brought back Shoko's spiteful face, but Rena chased it from her mind, laughing it off. She didn't know what had become of Shoko since then, but such a boring, stupid person had to be having a boring, stupid twentieth year. Rena set her glass down on the counter and opened the built-in fridge. She poured some Campari and grapefruit juice over the ice in her glass, stirring the cubes with her glittering nails, which faded from black to purple. She watched happily as the pretty red and yellow liquids blended together among the clinking ice.

It was an unusual color. She could see logic melting slowly into instinct. She took a sip and, satisfied with the flavor, lightly licked the traces of alcohol off her nails.

"I'm having another, too."

Rena slowly turned toward the male voice on her right, arranging her face into a smile. It was Jimmy, another of the participants. In his late twenties, he wore his dyed-brown hair in a soft, contemporary style. Each time he moved, a faint scent of vanilla wafted toward her.

"Oh, Jimmy-san," she said sweetly, scooting over to make room for him at the counter. The gesture was partly habit, partly a sign of her acceptance of his overture. At any rate, Jimmy was a popular YouTube commentator. He was probably the most famous person at the meetup. She gloated silently over the fact that he'd approached *her*, not the other way around.

"What're you drinking? Looks girly," he said smoothly in that same voice Rena knew from his videos. She threw him a vulnerable look.

"This? Campari and grapefruit."

"I see."

"Want a sip?" she asked casually, as if they were old friends. She held out the glass she'd already taken a few sips from. He reached for it, smiling at her willingness.

"Sure, why not?"

"Here you go."

He took the glass from her with an equally familiar gesture and gulped down a mouthful. Rena gazed at him with satisfaction.

"Like it?" she asked flirtatiously. She detected a glint of curiosity in Jimmy's eyes. She had a physical sense for what she needed to do in order to pique men's interest.

He held the glass up, clinking the ice cubes, and smoothly replied, "Not very strong."

"Wow, heavy drinker?" she said, taking a step into his personal life while at the same time brushing his back with her hand, as if to whisper to an even more personal side of him. He smiled casually, then took a few more sips of her drink, like it was his own. The glass was already half empty.

"This is good. Tastes like juice."

"That's my drink, you know."

"Oh right, I forgot."

He's acting friendly because he thinks my face is pretty, and he wants to touch my body, and I smell good, and he thinks he can pull this off. He knew nothing about who she was as a person, but she much preferred his attitude to false compliments. He followed his instincts straight toward her body. Plus, he was the most famous person in the room. She looked at his profile, a teasing smile on his lips, and thought, *I'd like to make him mine tonight.*

"Hey!" she said, caressing his shoulder lightly. He flinched, a jolt of electricity running through him at the ticklish sensation. The sight of it turned her on.

"Now, now," he said soothingly, setting his hand on her bare shoulder. Skin met skin, and warmth passed between them.

"You're burning up!"

"I am? It's because I'm drunk," she said, giggling teasingly and letting out a sexy sigh. She directed a melting gaze straight at him.

"Jimmy-san?"

Suddenly, another woman appeared next to him. It was Vanilla, another female participant, with an empty glass in her hand. Rena and Jimmy removed their hands from each other and looked at her.

Her hair was cut in a heavy bob, and she was wearing fluffy, girly clothes. Rena knew she was participating in the meetup as a musician who performed in videos. A few minutes earlier, while Rena and Jimmy were talking, she'd been watching them from a far table with distaste. Inumaru, the other female participant, was standing next to Vanilla, also giving Jimmy unhappy looks. Inumaru had dyed-blond hair and was dressed in a somewhat gaudy ensemble of primary colors.

"What's with you two?" Jimmy asked a bit grumpily.

"Jimmy-san, should you really be doing that? Your girlfriend will be mad," Inumaru whispered at him.

Jimmy frowned and glanced at Rena. Rena had heard what Inumaru said and was staring at her, expression unchanged.

"Did you come over here just to say that?"

"Well, she's my friend, too..."

Jimmy and Inumaru started arguing in hushed voices.

"I haven't even done anything yet!"

"Yet! See, I knew it!"

Rena sighed at the cold water being thrown on her evening, picked up her glass from the counter, and walked toward the middle of the room. She wasn't interested in getting pulled into whatever mess was brewing.

"Excuse me, Rena-san?" Vanilla said in an obviously hostile tone.

"Hmm? ...What is it?" Rena answered, not hiding her irritation. Vanilla walked over to her.

"Are you after Jimmy-san?" she asked quietly so Jimmy and Inumaru couldn't hear.

"...What?"

"It's disgusting the way you're trying to seduce him when there are so many fans who'd like to spend time with him."

Rena frowned in exasperation. The criticism was so childish, it reminded her of the spat with Shoko. Jealous women were all the same.

"What's that supposed to mean? Are you one of his fans?"

"No..."

"This is a meetup for gamers. I didn't think fans were allowed."

People like Vanilla always blamed someone else when they thought the thing they wanted was going to be stolen. They took no responsibility whatsoever for their own lack of desirability. Rena thought people like that, especially women, were pitiful.

"...Ugh," she sighed.

"What's with your attitude? How old are you anyway?"

"I'm twenty."

"I'm twenty-five. Don't you find it strange that you're ignoring a warning from an older woman? No one wants to see this."

Rena was thoroughly bored by Vanilla's increasingly heated words.

"So are you a fan or what? It's fine—you don't have to hide it. There are lots of people like you out there."

"...I am not..."

Rena figured she'd probably been nursing a wound ever since Jimmy approached Rena. She detested jealous liars like her.

"If you want him, all you have to do is the same thing I'm doing," she said venomously.

"You're disgusting…and anyway, he has a girlfriend."

Rena snickered, hoping her disdain would carve Vanilla's heart right out of her chest.

"You can't do it, can you?" Rena said, taking a step toward her and reaching out to pinch her stomach through her airy dress.

"What are you…?"

"You let yourself go and try to cover it up with fluffy clothes. Of course you can't!"

"…You bitch!"

Rena ignored her furious response, but the other participants seemed to have finally noticed the storm clouds developing in the corner.

"What's wrong, you two?" one of them said, stepping in to mediate.

"Come on, let's have a drink and make up," another said. The men were gathering around them in a panic.

"Whatever," Rena said flatly and walked off.

* * *

Fifteen minutes or so later, Jimmy was sitting at a table with another participant, apparently having finished his argument with Inumaru. Rena noticed him, but she didn't approach him, partly because her little fight with Vanilla had been so annoying. More than that, though, she knew he'd come back eventually.

"Rena-san, mind if I sit here?"

"Go right ahead."

So she killed time aimlessly talking to the insignificant men, who approached her completely unprovoked, and filled herself with alcohol. Really, she wasn't so much killing time as putting on a performance.

If you don't take me, someone else will.

While you're looking away, I might vanish.

Another fifteen minutes or so passed. Whether from irritation or impatience she didn't know, but Jimmy finally walked over to her with a glass in his hand.

"Sorry about earlier."

"Oh, that? It's fine."

He sat down next to her and tapped his glass lightly against hers. They shared the quiet *clink*.

"I didn't mean for you to have to listen to that."

"I know." Rena brought her face close to his. "So you have a girlfriend?" Her voice was colder than it had been before.

"Oh…well, we're not public about it."

"Hmm."

She placed her hand softly over his where it rested on the chair. Little by little, their warmth began to spread into each other again.

"…"

She smiled seductively and whispered breathily into his ear.

"But you came over to me again?"

She wrapped her fingers around his like tentacles, her gesture as suggestive as her words. Her caress lit a match to his instincts. Their entwined fingers were more honest than anything else, and both were equally hot.

"Didn't you want me to come over?" Jimmy asked, holding back his excitement even as his fingers continued to move against hers, devouring the sensation. She knew his mind must be full of what came next. So was hers.

"Maybe I did."

"I thought so."

Jimmy let go of her hand and wrapped his arm around her waist. She could feel his muscular, masculine build through her sweater. It was an indescribably pleasant sensation, knowing she'd made a place for herself in this valuable realm that the liars with their lily-white masks would never reach. She was enjoying her flirtation with Jimmy to the full.

"Yes, this is what I wanted to do," she said, touching his leg underneath the table, as close to the hip as she could get away with. His expression didn't change, but she sensed his body tense.

"Hmm? What's the matter?" she asked.

"…Nothing."

He was still pretending to be unmoved, but his excitement was obvious to Rena. His grip on her waist grew tighter, and both of them had broken out in a light sweat.

"Really? I thought I felt you twitch," she said, sliding her hand inward. His grip grew even tighter as he pulled her close.

"Mmm…," she said, much more coquettishly than before, leaning her upper body against him slightly. "Jimmy-san, you feel hot."

Instead of answering, he slid his hand up to her side, pressing in slightly for a better sense of the softness and curve of her waist.

"So do you."

"But in my case, it's because I'm drunk."

"Well, so am I."

Simply by moving in a tiny bit closer, she was able to break down the pretense of having everything under control and brush up against his more primal instincts. Using her femininity as a weapon, she grabbed hold of the part of him that could not resist and held his interest.

And he was the most famous person in the room.

He was a powerful branch to land on.

"…Are you now?"

She gazed at him with her sultry eyes; it felt like they were melting into a single unit.

"So then…we're both drunk?" she said, pouring the rest of her cocktail down her throat. A pleasant warmth spread through her brain, the alcohol washing away her logical self.

"That we are."

She could hear loud, happy voices in the background. She gave herself over to the tingly feeling in her hips, and the intoxication in her head, and the quiet, calm voice in her ear. She could feel her instincts slipping beyond her control. Finally, with a sense that they were both falling, she said it.

"Let's go to your place."

* * *

"See you later," Rena said, drying off her hair and leaving his house. The sun was already rising, and the thought of getting caught in the morning rush depressed her slightly. Some of the muddy snow was still lingering along the side of the road leading to the station. Rena glanced at it, tried stomping on it once, and was immediately bored.

When she got to the station, she sat down and checked her Twitter account. Opening up the message folder in her private account for mutuals, she found ten or eleven follow requests from guys she'd met at the meetup the previous night.

"Ah-ha-ha. That's a lot!" she said happily to herself as she accepted them one after another. Honestly, she didn't know who was who. But the fact that so many guys were interested enough in her to go to the trouble of sending a request pleased her.

But even better than that…

She looked at Jimmy's name in her list of followers. He only followed two hundred or so accounts, even though thirty or forty thousand people followed him. When she thought about the fact that she was among the less than 1 percent who got to be mutuals, she began to shake with excitement. She wondered how many of those two hundred were women he'd had a relationship with. She felt as if her identity as a woman had been affirmed by the numbers.

Rena slowly recrossed her legs below her sweater dress. That alone was enough to make men aware of her. Just then, her phone buzzed with a Twitter message notification.

"Huh?"

She was surprised to see it was a follow request—from the very same Vanilla she'd bickered with the night before. She thought about it for a moment, then figured it out.

"…She couldn't let it go."

She must have been unable to ignore the fact that Rena and Jimmy had left together. After all, she'd been quite stuck on him. Rena scrolled through Vanilla's account and found a bunch of tweets praising Jimmy's work as a commentator.

"Aha…I knew she was a fan. Liar."

She giggled. If another girl lied, all she had to do in return was tell the truth. So at eight o'clock that morning, half playfully and half provocatively, she sent the following tweet:

Heading home now.

Ten minutes or so later, Jimmy liked the tweet. Only then did Rena accept Vanilla's follow request.

5

All together now

Bottom-Tier Character Tomozaki

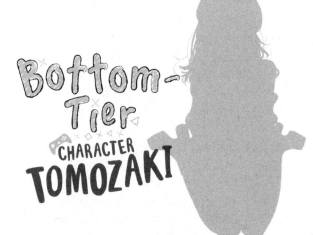

It was the end of the year, and the snow that had fallen around Christmas was beginning to melt. I was at Karaoke Sevens, where I work part-time. But I wasn't there to work.

"Yesss!! Are we gonna sing or what?! Are we gonna party?!"

Takei was standing in front of everyone in our room, shouting into a mic.

That's right. It was the day of the karaoke party with Nakamura's group, Hinami, Mimimi, Izumi, and me. The failed karaoke attempt following the Christmas party had been resurrected as an end-of-the-year party with the seven of us.

"Shut up, Takei!"

"You're being so loud!"

Oddly, Takei seemed to be enjoying the insults from Nakamura and Mizusawa. I think he likes any kind of attention.

"And he's right to! Brace your ears!"

Mimimi went right along with Takei's hyperactivity—of course, without a drop of alcohol in her system. She was holding another mic and standing near him. Considering that they were this excited before the singing even started, I had a feeling that I was about to be left in the dust. But this time, I couldn't let that happen. Because...

...Hinami had given me another assignment.

"There they go again," she said, turning to smile at me from her seat across from Mizusawa, who was next to me. Izumi was next to her, and Nakamura was next to Izumi, defending his girlfriend.

"Seriously. Hey, Fumiya...we've never done karaoke together outside of work, right?" Mizusawa said.

"Uh, actually...you're right."

Strictly speaking, I'd never done karaoke with friends before, but I decided not to say that. Hinami shot me a warning glance, then looked down and started fiddling with the electronic songbook. I've hardly ever done karaoke for fun, but I know one of these is called a *denmoku*. I do work here, so I know the lingo.

My assignment for the day was to sing at least one song with each person there.

I've gotten kind of close with these people, and part of me just wanted to enjoy the party, but I also know that complacency is the mortal enemy of any gamer who's aiming for the top. Overall, I was grateful for the assignment.

"I'm gonna do a Momoclo song!" Mimimi shouted, choosing her song before anyone else. Pictures from the Momoiro Clover Z song "Let's Go! Thief Girls" started to play on the screen. Mimimi stood in front of everyone and transformed into a star, throwing kisses at her audience. Well, at least she was having fun. Takei and the other guys were loving the show. Having Mimimi along for stuff like this really makes it fun. The music started to play, and she sang along, happily swaying back and forth.

"Reni, Kanako, Mimimi, Shiori, Ayaka, Minami. ♪"

"Hmm, I don't think that's in the original..."

"Wait, how are there two Mimimis?"

Everyone was getting a kick out of her sloppy lyrical change-ups, along with Nakamura and Mizusawa's teasing. Maybe because her voice is so loud to start with, the performance came off as simple and good, complete with little asides and fun gestures. She could probably do a great ballad without even messing around.

By the way, in the middle of the song there was a lyric that went "Numbers!" and then Mimimi pointed at everyone in turn.

"One!"

"Two!"

"Three!"

"Huh?"

"Five!"

"Whoo-hoo!"

Where did they all instantly learn what to say? Not in school, that's for sure.

"Last time!" she shouted at the end, then she sang out "Yuzu, Aoi, Mimimi, Hiro, Shuji, Fumiya ♪," which was nice, but then Takei got all sad and asked where his name was. Even though my name was just part of the list, I jumped when she said it. *Enough with the sudden attacks, okay? Mizusawa and my parents are the only ones who call me Fumiya.*

"Nice job!" Izumi said when Mimimi finished singing, grabbing a spare tambourine and shaking it.

The initial tidal wave was starting to knock me off my feet, but I had a job to do. Since this was my first time doing karaoke with friends, I didn't even know if I should act excited or talk to people, and now she'd added something on top of that. This felt like kind of a high bar, more along the lines of solving a puzzle than using my communication skills as a weapon.

"Okay! My turn!" Takei said, grabbing the mic and starting to sing "Love So Sweet" by Arashi. Takei is really built—definitely not someone who'd get scouted by any famous boy band talent agencies—so I could only conclude he was an Arashi fan. Just an ordinary guy who likes hamburgers, the Shinkansen, and Arashi, I guess.

As I watched him sing enthusiastically, something occurred to me. If I was going to sing a duet with everyone, I needed to create a duetty sort of mood. And it would probably be easiest to create that mood with Takei.

I looked at the *denmoku*, my mind racing. I needed a song I knew... that Takei also liked. As of now, I knew that he liked pork chop curry, space shuttles, and Bangiras.

Which meant...

I picked up the *denmoku* from the table, searched for the song I wanted, and pulled up the request screen. While Takei's song was in its interlude, I submitted the request. Then I sat back and waited for my prey to fall into the trap.

"Ooooh! Awesome choice!" Takei shouted excitedly as the song title appeared in the upper right of the screen. That was easy. So easy, the hunt was barely exciting.

"Oh, you like this song, Takei?"

"I love it! Damn, you stole it...," he said dejectedly.

That's right—I'd chosen "We Are!" one of the most popular theme songs from the anime version of *One Piece*.

"Wanna sing it together, then?"

"Really? Can I?"

"Of course, no problem," I said, successfully reeling in the first of my seven assignment targets. Of course, this was kind of a test run, and the others would likely be harder. I mean, I hardly know any songs to start with.

After Takei finished his song, a number by the artist AAA called "Rainy Skies and Love Sound" came on. I'd never heard of the singer or the song. Izumi took the mic, and I realized how different our musical universes were. By the way, Izumi is an amazing singer, with that normie power to her voice. It was a totally commonplace song with a bridge I vaguely recognized, but thanks to her talent, it sounded enjoyably musical.

Next up was "We Are!" Oh crap. I had Takei up there with me, but still, I'd never sung in front of classmates before. I was getting nervous. As I anxiously stood there, holding the mic, Takei said to me in a totally relaxed tone, "Our turn, Farm Boy. Can I do the thing?"

"The thing?"

"The thing at the beginning! Oh, wait—it's starting. I'll just do it!"

"Huh?"

I watched him, still not understanding, as he began intoning in a low voice:

"—Uh, wealth, fame... King...uh, Roger, got everything the world had to offer! And his words drove countless people to the sea! My treasure? Search for it! I left everything gathered together in one place! Just...find it!"

Even me, not your biggest *One Piece* nerd, could tell he'd totally messed up the intro narration and left a bunch of downtime at the end. I didn't know what to do, so I just stood there holding the mic. Takei didn't have anything to say either, which made for a fairly awkward moment.

"If you don't know the words, don't do the song!" Mizusawa shouted with a grin, which actually saved our butts. On the other hand, Takei's epic screwup helped me relax slightly.

We managed to make our way through most of the duet. *Now that I think about it, it's kind of sad. My karaoke duet virginity was stolen by Takei. Am I okay with that?*

"~~♪"

One upside was that since he was singing so loud, no one could hear my voice. I was still super nervous, though.

The song reached its last bridge. Everyone knew the song, and Takei was singing at the top of his lungs, which made for a generally rowdy atmosphere. When it finally ended, I let out a long breath. For a moment, the room was silent as the list of reserved songs popped up on-screen. *That moment between songs is so awkward. I didn't notice it after Izumi finished singing, but when my own song ended, I had a very strong urge to say something like, Sorry to make you suffer through that...*

Mizusawa must have noticed my strained expression, because he smiled confidently and thumped my shoulder. "Not as bad as I expected!"

"Yeah? Thanks."

"Of course, Takei was so loud, I could hardly hear you."

"Hey!"

By then, the next song had started to play. Guess that's the deal with karaoke—every couple of minutes you have a few seconds to talk.

"Lucid Dreamer" by ONE OK ROCK came up on the screen, and Nakamura took the mic. Hey, even I knew this one!

"Nice choice!" Izumi said happily, and Nakamura nodded back, actually looking semi-interested. *What a nice couple.*

He started singing. Turns out his singing voice is as powerful as the rest of him. He blasted his way through it like a rock star even though that high register had to be hard to sing. *Infinite potential, this one.*

At a few points, he stood up to sing more zealously or do some bad-boy moves. *He's got an almost childish side that comes out at these moments. At the same time, song selection does seem to reflect personality—in this case, a powerful song for a powerful guy. If I tried to sing something like that, I'd probably be drowned out by the backup singers.*

"Shuji's awesome!" Takei said, whipping up the crowd by grabbing the tambourine Izumi-style and starting to shake it. The role fit him so well I had to laugh.

"...Sounds like the tambourine is Takei's instrument," I said. Mizusawa sniggered from beside me.

"Thanks, dude!" Takei said happily, even though I hadn't meant it as a compliment. Oh well, that's fine.

Mizusawa took the mic next, and "Pretender" by Official Hige Dandism started to play. That song is super famous, and even I know the band's name is weird.

"Ooh, here it comes! Hiro's version of 'Pretender'!!"

Izumi, who until then had been cuddling up to Nakamura, seemed very excited about this development.

"I've been waiting for this!" Mimimi said.

"Yeah, it's not karaoke without this one," Hinami added excitedly. Guess he sings it every time. Reminds me how close they all are.

The song started playing. In contrast to Nakamura's display of power, Mizusawa took the smooth approach. The song seemed like another tough one, but he made it sound easy. His voice was fresh and sweet, the kind that everybody likes. Powerful Nakamura, skillful Mizusawa, and then Takei—everyone in this normie group had their distinct personality.

"Wow…"

Izumi gazed dreamily at the screen. I glanced at Nakamura. He looked very unhappy. You can read that guy like a book.

Now I was at a loss for what to do. I'd tried to set the stage for future duets by singing with Takei, but we'd just heard two solos. At this rate, completing my assignment was going to be tough.

Just then, however, the mood shifted.

"Mimimi, it's our turn!" Hinami said in the moment of silence between songs. I looked at the screen. "Chocolate Disco" by Perfume was up next.

"Here we go! We've got this!" Mimimi said excitedly. They seemed to have some secret plan. The two of them stood up and walked to a spot in front of everyone. Everyone clapped and I heard an "Ooh, I can't wait!" The intro came on—and the two of them started dancing.

"What the…?"

I smiled wryly. They were doing the same moves as the band members on-screen, perfectly synchronized. What was with these people?

They looked like total pros, singing along without even looking at the lyrics while performing their impeccable dance. *Come on, ladies, what is this? Do you do this every time?*

"You guys are so cute!"

"You're amazing at that!"

Izumi and Takei were both going wild, and Nakamura and Mizusawa were grinning, too. What the heck? I mean, sure, if two people this good-looking and athletic sing and dance, it's going to be fun to watch, and even I couldn't help staring. Plus, they were both good dancers.

Then I realized something. I thought the duet mood had fizzled, but everyone had been putting in their requests all along. Given the timing, Hinami must have put hers in while Takei and I were singing. With karaoke, there's a lag between creating a mood and that mood materializing. Maybe Hinami had taken mercy on me when she saw me singing with Takei and contributed in her own way.

Anyway, it would be easier to do another duet now. I figured I'd seize the opportunity by asking either Izumi or Mizusawa, who were sitting on either side of me.

But how? I couldn't think of a song that I knew I could sing with Izumi, and inviting her wouldn't be easy under Nakamura's watchful eye. Seeing her swoon over Mizusawa's performance a few minutes ago was enough to make him grumpy, so I have no doubt he'd chew me up and spit me out if he caught me inviting her to sing. I'd have to find a chance to do it undercover when he was singing or something.

I therefore decided to approach Mizusawa first. The vital question was, what song? I opened the "Top Hits" page on the *denmoku*, selected the "Duets" subcategory, and started scanning the list for something I knew that Mizusawa might get on board with. *Aha, found one!*

"…Mizusawa?"

"What?"

I showed him the *denmoku*. "Wanna sing this?"

"Together?"

"Yeah."

"Sure, but you just sang a duet."

My heart skipped a beat. When you're choosing your moves to achieve specific assignments, Mizusawa's sharp eye is downright terrifying.

"I d-did?"

"Surely now, Fumiya…"

"Wh-what?"

He grinned and pointed at me as I sat there anxiously.

"You're not embarrassed, are you?"

"Who, me?"

His guess was reasonable, especially given it would be virtually impossible for him to figure out that I was working on an assignment. Reassured, I moved on with my battle plan.

"Yeah. That's why I asked you."

"You're hopeless."

He smoothly snatched the *denmoku* out of my hands and entered our song request. It's probably just a habit of his to seize the leadership role in situations like this. Confident I was in good hands, I sat back and let him take over.

By the way, as we were working this out, Nakamura and Izumi were performing "AM11:00" by HY. It was so revoltingly flirty that I could see why some people want normies to die in a fire, and I'd rather not even mention it. But Izumi's harmonies during the bridge were so beautiful and Nakamura's rapping so outstanding it kind of got to me in spite of myself. I'd never heard the song before, but their version was so good I figured they must have sung it together at karaoke a bunch of times before. Which is stomach churning, so I think I'd rather skip it after all.

Mizusawa's and my turn rolled around. We were singing "Gray and Blue" by Kenshi Yonezu and Masaki Suda. It was famous enough to be familiar to me—and, needless to say, Mizusawa.

"Oooh, the Mizu-Tomo Band!" Mimimi called out mysteriously.

"Ha-ha-ha, what's that about?" Mizusawa answered, smiling wryly. I was too nervous to say anything.

"I'll sing first."

"Huh?"

As the first line began, I realized something—unlike my duet with Takei, this one didn't involve both of us singing at the same time. We had to take turns. Which meant the whole group was about to hear me do a solo. Now I was even more nervous.

Right now, there was a spade symbol over the lyrics. When it turned into a clover, it was my turn to sing. I know this stuff since I work here.

"♪♪♪"

Mizusawa sang the first line, then the second line, and then it was my turn— *Wait, what? Where is it?* With the spade still over the lyrics, the song went into the bridge, and then the bridge ended. Apparently, the song was divided into parts by verse. Which meant my voice was going to carry the entire second verse. I knew that when I signed up to do karaoke, but the prospect was still a little embarrassing.

"♪♪♪"

Nevertheless, I sang my part, glancing around the group to see their reactions. Some people were looking at the *denmoku*, others were watching the screen, and no one seemed to be having an extreme reaction to my performance. Someone had even gone to the drink bar for refills. Such is life.

We finished the song without incident, and I put down the mic. Hinami came up to me, smiling.

"Tomozaki-kun, you were really good!"

Was she talking about the assignment or my performance?

"Oh, thanks."

I glanced around the room. Apparently, she was going to sing something with Nakamura, because they were both holding mics. Now was my chance!

"Midday Sun" by King Gnu started playing. I knew that song, and I also vaguely remembered that it involved one singer with a high voice and one with a low voice. That's probably how they'd split up the parts.

Hinami started singing—and the mood changed. She'd shifted gears from "Chocolate Disco" to something more sincere. Filled with sighs and falsettos and vibratos, her rendition was practically at the level of a cover. I swear, she really is good at everything… Nakamura seemed like a fairly good singer in his own right, but even he was somewhat upstaged by Hinami.

I watched this duet between group leaders for a minute or two—then, at an opportune moment, I glanced at Izumi. Just like during what he'd done when Mizusawa was singing, she was pouting slightly. This was my chance.

"…Izumi?"

"Hmm? …Oh, Tomozaki!"

"Wanna sing something together?" I asked, loud enough for her to hear me over the music.

"Really? Sure!"

That was easy. I felt like it had more to do with her general enthusiasm than her jealousy toward Nakamura, but whatever—she said yes. The next problem was what song to sing. As I looked at the "Top Hits" page again, inspiration struck. I'd found it when I stopped searching within her territory and started poking around in my own territory for something she would know. I pointed to the *denmoku*.

"How about this?"

"…Ooh, *Demon Slayer*!"

That's right. I chose "Gurenge" by LiSA. Anime is its own world, but now and then, an insanely popular hit becomes a bridge between nerds and normies. *Demon Slayer* is the perfect example. I bet even Takei and Nakamura watch it, which is saying a lot. By the way, just because I'm a gamer doesn't mean I'm some expert on anime. Still, I know this kind of song better than that sparkly nonsense Izumi likes to sing. Also, this one was at the top of the list of anime songs, which just goes to show it can be dark at the foot of a lighthouse. I should have looked there first.

"I love that song! Let's do it!"

"Sounds good."

I input our request, thinking I'd safely cleared the hurdle of singing a duet with Izumi, when…Nakamura, approaching an interlude in his song, noticed my request and latched on to it.

"*Demon Slayer*, cool. Whose song is that?"

I got a sinking feeling.

"Me and Tomozaki!"

"What?"

He scowled at us. He looked super pissed, in fact. *Shit.* Just then, the interlude ended, and he started singing again, giving me a brief window of thinking time. If I didn't come up with a solution quick, he'd grind me up for dinner. But what to do? I strongly suspected that if I didn't do anything, he'd say he wanted to sing, too, and grab the mic, obstructing my assignment. Actually, not just a strong feeling—I was certain that's what he'd do.

I was in a tight spot. But I am nanashi, Japan's top gamer.

In which case, I should be able to come up with a way of turning the table. I hadn't wanted to show off my nanashi skills at a time like this, but I had no choice. Nakamura's face was so scary, I reflexively went into serious battle mode. My survival instinct kicked into gear. It didn't take long for me (as nanashi) to come up with a solution.

That's right—I changed a tight spot into an opportunity.

As soon as Nakamura finished singing, I leaned forward and said loudly enough for both him and Izumi to hear, "How about the three of us pass the mic around?"

"That sounds fun!" Izumi said, hopping on board right away.

Nakamura's face went blank for a second, then he gave in and said, "Fine." He probably figured it was better than the two of us doing a duet together.

Nice. I'd not only stopped him from stealing my hard-won chance to sing a duet with Izumi, I'd also managed to check off two names on my list at once. Hinami never said I had to sing a separate song with every person. Right, Hinami-san?

I ended up looking like the third wheel in a duet between Nakamura and Izumi, but we got through the song. Since Hinami wasn't part of the assignment, that left Mimimi.

But in a sense…she was the hardest one of all.

Most karaoke duets are love songs, and lots of songs are about love to

start with anyway. I couldn't put Mimimi in the position to sing something like that right now. She'd told me she liked me, and then I'd started
dating Kikuchi-san. I wasn't even sure it would be right for us to sing
together at all right now.

I glanced at the clock. We had around half an hour. At the current
pace, I probably had one or two more turns left. Maybe because the party
was winding down, the mood was calmer now. Hinami sang "Marigold"
by Aimyon, which set off a string of mellower songs. Mimimi sang "Unfit
for Love" by Koresawa, and Izumi sang "366 Days" by HY, and by then,
the atmosphere felt really nice. It was like everyone was singing meaningful stuff. Of course, I was at a total loss for what to do. Obviously, I don't
have a special meaningful song.

Now Mizusawa was singing "Sparkle" by RADWIMPS, and once
again Izumi was watching dreamily while Nakamura scowled. This was
turning into such a standard routine, I wasn't even worried anymore. By
the way, before Mizusawa, Takei sang another one by Arashi. Well, nothing wrong with that.

While Mizusawa was singing, Nakamura was scrolling furiously through
the *denmoku*. After lengthy consideration, he selected "Wherever You Are"
by ONE OK ROCK. I wondered what took him so long, but he was probably just looking for a song he could use to compete with Mizusawa.

"♪♪"

The careful selection process was evidently worthwhile, because
Nakamura's "special song" was super sappy, and Izumi was swooning in
her seat. Fine, they're a couple—whatever—but I wish they'd leave the
rest of us out of it. I'd seen too much already.

Meanwhile, we were down to ten minutes before we had to leave.
There was only time for one or two more songs. This was definitely my
last chance. The only person left on my assignment list was Mimimi.
What should I do? I'd been thinking about it while everyone sang their
special songs.

How could I set up the right situation for us to sing together? Would
it be awkward? I ran through various possibilities in my head and decided
to take a gamble.

I touched the *denmoku* screen, submitting my request.

The words "Choral song: Leaving on a Journey" appeared on the kara-oke screen. I watched to see how everyone reacted.

"...Oh, nice one, Brain!!"

"Awesome, Farm Boy! I'm in!"

I'd successfully hooked Mimimi, as well as Takei, who I'd suspected might fall for my ploy as well.

"Should we all sing it together?" Izumi asked.

This was exactly what I'd hoped for: an ensemble number that we all sang together.

Working here, I've observed groups of students finish up their sessions like this a number of times. I could see how this would get us going more than a solo as the last song. Plus, I'd achieve my assignment of singing with Mimimi. After all, I'd sung with Nakamura and Izumi as a three-some, so I already knew it didn't have to be a duet. Call me sly, but it's really Hinami's fault for leaving a loophole in the rules.

Anyway, we all sang the song, which means I sang with Mimimi and my assignment was complete... Right, Hinami-san?

Mizusawa and I had shifts at Karaoke Sevens after that, so we stuck around while everyone else left. Now that I thought about it, even though I'd been struggling to get my assignment done for several hours, doing karaoke with a group of friends was pretty fun.

Mizusawa and I went into the changing room to kill time until our shift started, and I composed a LINE message to Hinami.

[*Since Mimimi was part of that last number, it counts as completing the assignment, right?*]

I sent the message off, feeling smug, then waited for her to respond. *Heh-heh, what do you say to that, NO NAME? This is how nanashi fights: by changing the rules.* I imagined her expression of defeat as I sat there waiting. After a few minutes, her response came.

*   *   *

[*Sure, it counts, but in that case, you could have just sung the one song and skipped all the others!*]

"…Doh."

Now that she mentioned it, I realized she was right. Since everyone sang together at the end, all my struggles to set up individual duets were meaningless.

"…Huh."

"What's up, Fumiya?"

"Oh, uh, nothing, nothing."

Even though I'd completed an assignment, a mysterious but unshakable sensation of defeat hovered in the back of my brain.

6

An angel in the *kotatsu*

Bottom-Tier Character Tomozaki

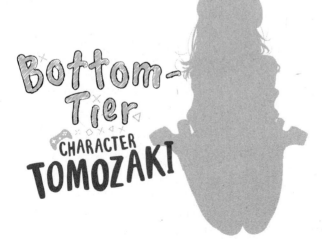

December 31. New Year's Eve.

I was sitting under the blankets of our *kotatsu* table at home, eating satsuma oranges. My head was filled with all the changes that took place this past year. For someone like me, who lived alone in a colorless world for most of my life, those changes have been almost too vivid. The dazzling colors and heart-shaking emotions were enough to take this shy girl's breath away, yet everyday life has become so much more fun.

What makes me happier than anything is knowing that it's not the world that's changed—but me.

So there I was, holding a piece of satsuma in one hand and my cell phone in the other. When did I start eating while I was on my phone? Isn't that bad manners? Well, I don't think I'd have experienced the excitement of waiting for a message notification unless I lived in this new world, and that feels important to me.

I had fruit in one hand, and my other hand was waiting for a sweet message.

This mix of happiness and anxiety feels unnatural, but I think in truth it's completely natural.

My world really has changed since the days when my inferiority complex and uncertainty piled up like snow, darkening my view. These days everything is so full of light.

And what caused this change? The person my left hand is waiting so eagerly to hear from.

"Fuka, Mom says she's not putting mochi in the soba noodles!"

My little brother Riku came running out of the kitchen and sat down next to me. He's in his first year of junior high, four years younger than me, but we're still as close as ever. It's hard to believe, since at school he's so outgoing he's even head of school spirit for Athletics Day. I think he shows a slightly different side of himself at home and at school. Everyone does that, even me—we have different selves for different situations.

"Mochi doesn't go in New Year's Eve soba!" I told him.

"Really? It doesn't?"

"No. It goes in the soup on New Year's Day."

"Ohhh, you're right!"

It's cute how easy it is to convince him of things. I stroked his hair affectionately. "Stop it!" he said, but he didn't try to escape, which makes me think he didn't actually hate it all that much.

"By the way, Mom just told me something!"

"What'd she tell you?"

"That you have a boyfriend! Gross!"

"What...?"

I can't believe he just said that. I knew he'd tease me about it, which is why I didn't tell him in the first place, but now that he found out, he's accusing me of things I'd never do!

"I am not gross!"

"But having a boyfriend means you do that stuff, right?"

"N-no...I haven't done anything yet..."

My face was getting unbelievably hot. Just imagining it makes me dizzy, but—

"Oooh, you said 'yet'!"

"R-Riku!"

He was right. What I said made it sound as if I assumed we'd do that stuff at some point. On the other hand, it's not as if it will never happen. I'd just been avoiding thinking about it.

"D-don't say that!" I scolded him.

"Eeew, you're so gross!"

"S-stop it!"

I don't have the chance to practice conversations like this at school very often, so he runs circles around me. I'm not sure what to do about it. I think this is something only boys talk about, so it's inevitable that I've

got a thin skin on the subject. Or maybe I'm just telling myself that so I don't feel bad.

"Riku! Come in here!" our mom called from the kitchen, having overheard our conversation.

"What?" he called back a little grumpily. He stood up reluctantly but nevertheless did as he was told. That's what's so cute about him.

"Oh, Fuka, are you having soba with us?" he asked as he was about to disappear into the kitchen.

"Yes!"

"How hungry are you? Should I give you a lot?"

"A normal serving is fine."

"Okay!"

With that, my mischievous, nosy brother went in to help our mom serve up the food. I started to tidy up the *kotatsu* table. Dad was shut up in his office because he said he needed to finish up some work, but he does that every year, so I'm sure he'll pop out half an hour before midnight.

It was already eleven. The year really was nearly over, and I could sense the new one approaching.

After checking the time, I set my phone facedown on the table and reached for the copy of *On the Wings of the Unknown* that was sitting next to it. As I flipped through it, red marks leaped out at me from every page. I'd marked it up with notes so that my directions during rehearsals would be clearer. Thinking back on it, I realized that everyone had been working hard to realize my own personal vision. That really was a gift. The script was evidence of that period in my life, and it was the most valuable treasure imaginable to me.

"Ah..."

My eyes happened to fall on a scene featuring Alucia, one of the heroines. The red notes mentioned Natsubayashi-san's direct gaze and Hinami-san's bloodcurdling performance. The story I'd created came together onstage in an unbelievably ideal way, and I'm certain it contained more than the characters themselves.

I'd been trying to convey something in that scene. I read through it again slowly.

*　　*　　*

"I don't think I have a favorite thing."

Alucia smiles sadly while speaking. Kris is flustered.

"What? I—I mean, you know so much! You're so good at making things, and you're even great at magic! I bet you like lots of things!"

"Not really. I've got royal blood, and one day, I have to be queen… That's the only reason I work so hard. It's not because I enjoy it."

"You said it's the only reason, but it's an amazing one! Compared with you, I don't have anything."

"That's not true."

"I want to be like you, Alucia."

Alucia frowns.

"—Like me?"

Alucia stares at Kris.

"I think your view of me is mistaken, Kris."

"It is?"

"I'm not the wonderful kind of person you think I am."

"What do you mean?"

"I have everything. But—"

Alucia turns to the audience.

"—that's exactly why…I have nothing."

As I read it, the performance of the scene streamed through my mind, like a scratch mark throbbing in my heart. The last line was particularly resonant. The vacancy of those words was like a knife, as if they contained the true Alucia—and even more. I felt as if Hinami-san herself had said those words.

Or maybe I'm not saying it accurately. After all, I included those lines specifically because I knew Hinami-san would be playing the role.

"I wonder if I got it right after all…," I mumbled, thinking back to the previous week.

Had I gone in too deep? I still didn't know.

*　*　*

"Fuka-chan?"

Hinami-san had approached me at the end of the party to celebrate the school festival, amid the happy chatter of our classmates and the savory smell of charred sauce at the *okonomiyaki* restaurant.

"...Hinami-san?"

I was quite surprised. On that day, I'd spoken with more people than usual, and I'd begun to feel I was learning to open up a little, but something about Hinami-san felt off when she came up to me.

"Great job today...and on the script."

"Um...same to you. Great job playing Alucia."

The two of us were standing apart from everyone else, in the hallway by the bathroom. She could have talked to me anytime during the party, but the fact that she started the conversation there indicated she wanted to talk alone.

"Thanks. The script was so good," she said smoothly, as if the thought had just occurred to her, but I suspected she'd planned to bring up the script from the start. I'm not sure why I thought that. Maybe it was an intuition, maybe an assumption, or maybe my own image of Alucia. Maybe even the things Hinami-san said when Tomozaki-kun and I interviewed her led me to that conclusion. Whatever the answer, I sensed something at that moment.

"Thank you so much. It was difficult to write...but I think it came out well."

"Ah-ha-ha. I'm glad to hear that."

She grinned and met my eyes. I'm not sure why—there was nothing whatsoever in her expression to suggest an ulterior motive—but it frightened me.

"I thought it was really interesting, too."

She hadn't said anything strange. But there was something in her tone—like the echo of water dripping in a dark cave. A loneliness, a feeling of isolation.

"Thank you...so much."

"I wanted to ask you about Alucia...," she continued, hardly waiting for me to finish my thank-you. Her expression was cheerful and happy and friendly, but at the same time, I didn't feel free to move away from her.

"Alucia is an empty person, isn't she?"

"...Yes."

"Interesting." She glanced down, then looked me in the eye again. "And she pours herself into various things because she's trying to fill that emptiness?"

"Yes."

The unexpected direction of the conversation startled me, and I tried to figure out her motivation for asking me these questions.

"I believe she said...that she had everything, which was exactly why she had nothing."

"...Yes, that's right."

She glanced down again and swiftly licked her lips.

"Well, I interpreted that line in my own way during the performance, but I was wondering what you meant when you wrote it."

Why was she asking me this? Of course, it could have been pure curiosity, but I sensed that wasn't the case. After all, I modeled the character on Hinami-san herself. When I created Alucia, I knew it might shake her...and perhaps a part of me even hoped that it would. The truth is, I was interested in the thoughts and emotions of this seeming sorceress who brought color to Tomozaki-kun's world—and in the face beneath her mask.

"Um..."

That's why I chose my words so carefully. For myself as well as for her, I wanted to explain my image of Alucia as accurately as possible.

"Alucia...has nothing that she truly likes, so she can't validate herself internally," I said, using the mask of the story's main character. "That's why she wants some kind of proof that she's on the right path."

"Proof?"

I nodded. "For example, it would be easy to believe that some made-up story proved her worth, but she's too strong for that and too smart... She can't believe in flimsy fairy tales."

"And that's why she strives to be the best in martial arts and academics?"

I nodded again. "...Yes. She finds meaning in the things that the world tells her are valuable."

"Interesting... I see."

She frowned, glancing away for a second. I can guess why, but I don't know the real reason.

"And...does Alucia realize that about herself?"

I hesitated for a moment, but I had an answer.

"I think...she does realize it. She knows she looks perfect from the outside, but in reality, she has nothing. That's exactly why she confesses the truth to Kris."

Hinami-san nodded, a satisfied look in her eye.

"So that's what those lines meant."

"...Yes," I said. "That's what it meant *about Alucia*."

She nodded silently several times before responding. "Why did she become like that? Why did she end up so empty, without anything she liked?"

Answering that question was slightly difficult. I didn't know why she was asking, for one thing, but the reason was only something I imagined for the story. Nevertheless, I tried to explain it to her as accurately as I could.

"I think...it's because she was born into the royal family."

"The royal family, huh?"

This was all in the realm of imagination. "She was born to be a queen, so everything she does is assigned an external value of good or bad."

I asked myself, if there was a girl somewhere in the world who was empty inside...

"She had to constantly ask herself, not 'what do I want to do,' but 'what is the correct thing for a princess to do?' That way of thinking was firmly rooted in her."

...What sort of environment could have produced that mental state and value system?

"I think the only goal she was able to find for herself was submitting to the rules of that world."

I tried as hard as I could to imagine, and to get to the deepest part of the character's heart.

"But when she stopped believing in that world, she was left with... nothing."

I tied all the pieces together in my own world and wove them into a story.

"So she ended up hollow inside..."

That was how I understood Alucia's *motivation*.

Hinami-san blinked in apparent surprise.

"...It's amazing that you thought so deeply about it." She glanced down pensively, then redirected her powerful gaze at me. "You said you did some interviews...didn't you?"

"Um...yes."

This was another unexpected turn in the conversation. She was asking about the interviews Tomozaki-kun and I conducted about her own past.

"Did you learn anything? About me...and my circumstances?"

What came to mind first was her younger sister. But we hadn't heard anything specific. Only that she'd had two younger sisters, who she was close with in elementary school, but by middle school, one of them had disappeared. I didn't know exactly what had happened, only that something surely had. I didn't know how open I should be, but I decided to tell her the truth.

"I heard that your younger sister—"

"You heard?"

Her voice ripped the air. I was truly shocked. The look on her face at that moment was exactly the same as Alucia's the first time she saw the dragon: sharp, unwavering, and strong enough to strangle me. Those eyes, so black they took my breath away, pierced my heart.

"N-no...only fragments and speculations..."

"What fragments?"

"Um...only that when we talked to your friends from elementary school and from junior high, they talked about different sisters..."

"...I see."

"I—I...I'm sorry... It's none of my business."

She stared at me expressionlessly for a moment, and very briefly, her black eyes wavered.

"Does Tomozaki-kun know?"

"...Yes."

"Really. I see."

That was all she said. After that, her usual expression returned.

"Oh, I'm sorry to bring this up so suddenly. The play really was wonderful! Excellent work, really!"

"Th-thank you."

"Well, I'll be off, then!"

She turned and walked away, leaving me feeling incredibly uneasy.

* * *

I looked down, realizing I'd dropped the piece of satsuma orange I'd been holding.

"Oops..."

Luckily, it fell onto the peel, so I picked it up, stared at it for a moment, then popped it into my mouth.

Thinking back on my conversation with Hinami-san had brought up a mix of emotions. I'd fleshed out Alucia's character with her in mind. Was it really the right decision to talk about her inner story with Hinami-san? Should we have conducted those interviews about Hinami-san's past, delving into her personal history? Once something was discovered, it couldn't be hidden again. What did she really think? Only she knew the answer to that question. But if you're going to poke around in someone's personal life, you have to be ready for the consequences. Had I thought enough about that beforehand?

"Fuka, the soba's ready!" Riku called from the kitchen, breaking my reverie. Returning to reality, I called back.

"Great, thanks!"

I went into the kitchen, and we each picked up two bowls of soba to bring back to the *kotatsu*. The fragrance of the smoky broth, the pieces of duck perched atop the warm noodles, and the wisps of steam rising from the bowls were the perfect accompaniment to the end of the year. Dad appeared from his room to join us, Mom came out from the kitchen, and the whole family settled in around the *kotatsu* table.

"What a year this was," Dad said.

"Yes, it certainly was a roller-coaster ride! To think that Riku became head of the school spirit squad and Fuka wrote a play for the school festival!" Mom added.

"I'm sorry I couldn't go to your play, Fuka. Was it a success?"

"Yes, it was. I have the script if you'd like to read it."

"I'd love to read it later. After work calms down a bit…maybe at the end of January…"

"Tee-hee. You sure are busy, Dad."

Moments like this with my family mean more to me than anything in the world.

After we ate our soba, we waited for the clock to strike twelve.

"Fuka, it's almost midnight!"

"Oh, you're right…twenty more seconds!"

In a prayerful mood, I watched the numbers count down on the TV screen. This really was a wonderful year—and that's why I wanted the next one to be even better.

And I wasn't just wishing—I was determined to make it that way.

With less than ten seconds left until midnight, Riku started shouting out the numbers excitedly.

"Four, three, two, one!"

"Happy New Year!"

All four of us clapped our hands, welcoming the new year. We do the same thing every year, but somehow, the scene this time seemed to be splashed with more color than usual.

"…Oh!"

Just then, my phone buzzed. I looked down.

*　　*　　*

[*Happy New Year, Kikuchi-san.*
I'm looking forward to visiting the shrine with you tomorrow.]

It was the LINE message from Tomozaki-kun that I'd been waiting for. I squeezed my phone.

"Ewww, you're acting so girly! Gross!"

"I t-told you…"

"Gross…?! Fuka, what is your brother talking about?" Dad asked.

"Riku, I told you to keep it a secret from your father!"

"A s-secret?! F-Fuka, what is this s-s-secret?!"

"Um…it's not…"

"What's n-n-not?!"

"Darn it, Riku!"

And so my New Year began, a little more chaotically than usual but full of exciting hopes.

I glanced out the window. In the light shining from inside, I saw that the heavy snow piled thickly on the garden had melted clear away.

Afterword

It's been a while. Yuki Yaku here.

Nearly four years have passed since I started this series, and here we are at the tenth volume, which certainly deserves celebration. I'd never have made it this far without the support from all you, my readers. As an author who's sold a million books, I extend my sincerest gratitude.

In addition, as the author of a series that's been adapted as an anime, I want to write even better stories in the future, which is to say, I believe it is my mission as an author who sells an average of a hundred thousand books per volume to convey as fully as possible the appeal of my characters.

Anyway, thank you! The *Tomozaki* series has broken the one million mark!

And that's not the only thing I have to celebrate. The special edition of this volume includes the first CD dramatization of the series, and in May, a spin-off manga featuring Mimimi as the main character will launch. The anime version has been officially announced and is getting closer to broadcast. The comic version is in progress as well. You can take your pick! I'm deeply grateful for all these developments.

As you might guess, with so much going on, these have been very busy times for me. In addition to the basic work of writing the story, I've had to learn to switch gears between everything from working on the audiobook and the manga to attending script meetings. You could say I'm traveling various roads parallel to the main road, or if you wanted to put it in terms of the first color page in this collection, you could liken my work to the delicate variations in the shades of black that the artist has used for the hair of the three Hinami sisters.

I can practically hear you saying, *There he goes again*, but just hear me out. What I want to emphasize is that all three girls are in elementary school in that picture—which means their hair has to be black, not dyed. Black absorbs all colors and has no color itself. One would think that as a result, creating variation would be difficult.

And yet take a look at that illustration. There's a brownish black, a bluish black, and a pinkish black. The shades are so fresh one would never call them the same simple *black*, but still they fall within the boundaries. What a splendid job the artist has done in distinguishing these colors. I hope you can see how this excellent depiction leaps effortlessly over the typical challenge of portraying sisters. Sisters are blood relatives. Although that doesn't necessarily mean they look alike, drawings of sisters tend to depict them that way. The picture of the three Hinami sisters is no exception. Although there are slight differences related to their ages, the key elements of their facial features and hairstyles have been drawn to resemble one another. The similar part in their bangs and color of their eyes is especially striking. They are sisters, so naturally, their standout features are similar.

You could say that the same thing goes for hair color. Realistically speaking, they're related, so they're all going to have black hair. In the world they inhabit, on the far side of the printed page, their hair is probably the exact same color. And yet, in the pages of this book, Fly-san has conjured up a splendid paradox.

Yes, that's right. In the world the three sisters inhabit, their hair is the same color, but when they are brought to life in our own world, the magic of color renders their black hair "the same but different."

And that is not the only noteworthy point. If I asked you which one was Aoi, who would you choose? ...I thought so. Somehow, you knew the answer. Of course, the text says she's the oldest sister, so perhaps you decided based on her height. But what if you didn't know that? Yes—you still would know which was her.

I bet you know why. It's because you've already got an image of Aoi Hinami as having that paradoxical pinkish-black hair, isn't it? And the paradox stands in this illustration. In other words, the artist has connected two isolated worlds through the use of color. A miracle in black.

I hope I've managed to communicate my thoughts. With that, I'd like to move on to something unusual—a note on one of the short stories in this collection. Specifically, I'd like to discuss the fact that I've never clearly stated the year in which the *Tomozaki* series takes place. The reason I didn't is because I wanted to depict a certain kind of fictionalized "now" that incorporates bits and pieces of the ever-evolving time we live in, as if the novel is constantly providing a window onto the present moment. However, in the story "All together now," the songs that the characters sing, along with their other words and actions, allow the reader to figure out more or less when the story takes place. Therefore, I'd appreciate if you could interpret it as a kind of parallel or hypothetical—a story about what would happen if this group of characters in their second year of high school happened to go out to karaoke at the point in time when this volume was published. Next year and the year after, they'd probably sing different songs at this same year-end party, right?

Now on to the acknowledgments.

To my illustrator Fly-san, Iwaasa-san is going to send you some macaron cookies, but don't eat them. I suspect they contain a poison designed to make you want to draw limitless quantities of illustrations. Also, I'm a big fan of yours.

To my editor Iwaasa-san, looks like I made the deadline with ease again this time, eh? Ha-ha. I'll try to do the same next time as well.

To my readers, I think you'll be surprised by the many new turns the plot is about to take. I hope you'll continue reading, because I'm really looking forward to expanding the story. Thank you for all your support.

Finally, beginning on the next page, you'll find a "bonus track": a short story version of the audiobook CD included with the special edition. Enjoy! I hope to see you again in the next volume.

Yuki Yaku

Bonus Track

The virtual reality adventure of Tomozaki the Warrior

Bottom-Tier
Tier
CHARACTER TOMOZAKI

I excitedly removed a machine about the size of my two hands from its box.

"So this is what the latest virtual reality headset looks like... It's lighter than I thought... Wow... So futuristic..."

I was holding what looked like a pair of oversized goggles in my hands. Apparently, Mizusawa had been selected as a beta tester, and our usual crew was supposed to play an online game today using these headsets. I was super excited to try out the latest VR game.

"We're all supposed to log on at five... Oh shit, it's already 5:02! ...So I guess I, uh, put this on my head and press that button?"

Muttering to myself, I slipped the headset on, felt around for the button on the side, and held it in for a few seconds. A futuristic sound blared near my ear.

"Wow!"

I passed through a gate made of light and emerged in an imaginary Western-style living room. When I moved my head, my view of the room changed exactly as it would if I were really right there, and the image quality was way higher than I would have expected for a goggle display. I felt like the technology was almost too advanced. How'd they even do this?

As I was going into shock over just how cutting edge this thing was, I suddenly heard Hinami's voice.

"...Hello?"

"H-hello...?" I answered timidly.

"That sounds like the Brain's voice! So you finally showed up!" I heard Mimimi answer.

"Sorry. That you, Mimimi?" I asked, a bit surprised by this barrage of voices. It seemed as if the space before my eyes was supposed to be my room in the game, and now other characters were there. Hmm. So we were supposed to be communicating by phone or ESP?

"You sure are late, Fumiya. Aren't you the guy who loves games?"

That was Mizusawa. His I've-got-everything-under-control tone came through loud and clear even over the headset. The ultimate top-tier character.

"Y-yeah, but I've never done VR before... I was geeking out over the gear, and I lost track of the time," I answered honestly.

"I swear, Tomozaki-kun, you're hopeless," Hinami said in a teasing tone. She sounded kind of like her real self, which was annoying, but I suppressed my irritation and apologized again. *Damn you, Hinami! I can't do anything now, but you better watch out later!*

"Ah-ha-ha. He likes games so much he was late!"

A new voice had joined the conversation: Izumi's.

"Oh hi, Izumi, you're here, too? I figured you wouldn't want to bother with the setup."

"Hey, what's that supposed to mean? My mom helped me out."

"Is that really something to brag about?" I teased, used to talking through the headset by now.

With most of us assembled, Hinami took the lead. "Hinami here. Who's ready to go?"

"Oooh, Takei here! Ready and eager!"

"Uh, Yuzu Izumi here! I can hear you!"

"Ha-ha-ha. You don't have to copy them, Yuzu."

"Um, is that so, Hiro?!"

"I'm ready, too. Come and get me!"

As everyone checked in, I heard a new, uncertain voice.

"Umm...can you hear me?"

"Yes, I can hear your adorable voice, Tama!"

"No need for the commentary!" Tama-chan shot back with her usual sharpness.

Mimimi giggled.

"Wow, this headset is incredible! I can't believe we can talk between houses like this!" Takei said, slightly out of step with everyone else.

"Uh, actually, you can do that on a phone," I answered.

"Geez, Takei... Anyway, is everyone ready?" Mizusawa asked.

"I sure am!" Mimimi answered. "I'm so excited to try VR for the first time! And the newest model, too!"

"So you're a tester for a game they're developing? You're so lucky!" I said.

"They must know I'm a cool guy."

"You're so annoying, Hiro!" Izumi said, laughing.

"But we can go inside the game, right?! Aren't you guys psyched?!" Takei said.

"They do seem to be using the latest technology. I have to admit, I'm excited, too," Hinami added.

"And it's an RPG with swords and magic, right?! That's, like, so exciting!" Takei answered.

Tama-chan laughed. "Ah-ha-ha. Yeah, I can see you liking that."

"I love it!"

I smiled wryly, then brought up something that I'd been wondering about.

"It feels so futuristic. I wonder if this'll mess with our brains."

"That's...a scary thought...," Izumi said. Just then, a bell chimed to announce a new participant.

"H-hello...?" said a beautiful, fleeting, fairylike voice.

"Oh, that sounds like the adorable Fuka-chan! I've been waiting for you!"

Hinami followed up Mimimi's exaggerated welcome with a gentler one. "Looking forward to the game!"

"Me too! Thank you for inviting me. I'm sorry to be late..."

"No problem! Did you have trouble connecting?"

"Um, no, I was able to connect... I just didn't know how to join the conversation..."

Mizusawa and Hinami jumped in to reassure her.

"Ha-ha-ha, I completely understand!"

"Yes, of course!"

"Hey, that's not the reception I got!" I joked, since they'd just scolded me for being two minutes late. I felt like all I was doing was making jokes.

"But what about Shuji? Since Fuka-chan is joining us, I really wish he could be here," Izumi said regretfully.

Mizusawa laughed. "He said he doesn't have Wi-Fi at home, so what can you do? It's an online game."

"Yeah, you really do need Wi-Fi for this. You'd burn through your data in a second otherwise!"

"All he ever uses his phone for is social media… Anyway, I think we're all here, right?" Mizusawa asked.

"Let's see…me, Yuzu, Tama-chan, Fuka-chan, Mimimi," Hinami said like she was taking attendance. "And then Takahiro, Takei, and Tomozaki-kun… Yup, that's everyone."

"Okay. Should we get started?" Mizusawa asked, taking the lead.

"Sounds good," Izumi answered.

"The game is on!"

"I'm looking forward to it!"

A start menu floated in front of my eyes with buttons like START GAME and OPTIONS.

"Okay, so I choose START GAME and…oh shit!!"

The second I made my selection, a tornado of light swallowed up the world.

* * *

"Uh, okay…ouch… Where am I?"

When the light receded, I was standing in an open meadow. Wind was blowing, rustling the grass. The graphics were way better than on most games, and when I moved, my avatar in the game moved in tandem, almost seamlessly. Wonder how it works.

"A meadow with nothing in it…?"

I heard a weird sound behind me, like a time warp, and then the sound of something heavy falling. I whirled around in surprise.

"Huh?"

Mimimi was sitting on the ground. She stood up, rubbing her butt. "Owww! Where am I...? Is that you, Brain?!"

"Hey, Mimimi... What are you wearing?"

"What?"

She was dressed in shorts and a tube top, with a green cape tied around her neck. She also had on elbow-length gloves and a small leather bag secured to a belt around her waist. Her legs and stomach were exposed, and she looked very, uh, fit.

I looked away from her as I answered, "You're dressed like a robber or something."

She looked down at herself.

"What the heck?! You're right! These shorts are barely there!"

"And you've got a bandanna or something around your head... They said this was an RPG, right?"

"Yeah."

"Which means you're a thief."

As I was talking, it finally occurred to me to look down at myself. I could see armor and a sword and shield. Classic RPG stuff.

"If I've got armor on...am I a soldier?"

"You like more like a warrior to me."

"S-seriously? Don't tell me I ended up as the main character!"

"Ah-ha-ha. You've always got the best luck." She thumped me on the shoulder.

"Not sure if it's good luck or bad..."

"Seriously, though, this game is amazing! We look totally different! It's almost too real!"

We looked around at the unbroken expanse of green.

"...But what is this place? A grassland?" Mimimi asked.

"Oh, I bet it's the meadow they typically have at the beginning of games. Seems like...we're the only ones around, huh?"

"Yeah. Does that mean we're the only two who started from here?"

"Seems like it... Hey, what was that?"

Just then, the grass rustled. I turned toward the sound and found a sticky blue monster hopping toward us and howling menacingly. Who knows where it came from.

"Pigii! Pigii!"

"Eee! A monster! It's all wobbly and gross!" Mimimi said.

"Uh, doesn't it kind of sound like Takei...?"

Even though there was some kind of effect on the voice, it did sound like him—or rather, it *was* him.

"Yeah, but what *is* he?"

"Well, this is the first monster to appear, and it's blue and wobbly... Sounds like slime to me."

"You're so calm, Brain!"

"Yeah. This is kind of a standard thing. I bet we're in the tutorial right now. There's no way we'll lose, so let's just relax, okay?"

"Doesn't that kind of take away from the fun?"

"What are you talking about? Analyzing the metagame is part of the fun these days."

"I have no idea what you're talking about, but really?"

I felt like a fish in water as I explained our situation. Mimimi seemed to only understand around half of what I said, but she crouched down and, from what I could tell, got ready to fight the monster we were facing. She's a natural.

"Pigii!"

"Ack! Oh boy, here it comes!"

"Let's do this!"

Our first battle began, along with an upbeat battle theme.

"Uh...how do we fight? I don't see any commands..."

"You called it a tutorial, but who's doing the tutoring?"

Just then, I heard a faint, kind voice.

"Tomozaki-kun! Nanami-san!"

Mimimi craned her neck around, confused.

"Where's that voice coming from?" I asked.

"Over here!"

"Where?" I scanned our surroundings, searching for the owner of the voice.

"On your shoulder!"

"My shoulder... Argh!"

Mimimi and I found her at the same time. A tiny Kikuchi-san, dressed in white and sporting a set of wings, was hovering over me.

"Are you a fairy that looks like Kikuchi-san?"

"Um...hello," the fairy said.

Mimimi and I returned her greeting.

"H-hi."

"Hello!"

"Um...my name is Fuka. I'm a fairy who helps everyone on their adventure...apparently," Kikuchi-san said hesitantly, flitting lightly around us. Just seeing her was enough to fill me with gratitude.

"I guess that's one way for the game to work..."

"Oh my god, she's so cute! She's even littler than Tama! So adorable!!"

"Uh, um, cute..."

"She could fit in my palm! I can't stand it! It's too perfect! Brain, starting today, I am Team Fuka-chan."

"Uh, okay..."

"Um...? Thank...you?"

Neither of us knew how to react to Mimimi's excitement—except for Takei, apparently. "Pigii!! Pigii!!"

"Takei... I mean, the slime is pissed off!"

"I think he's upset because we're not including him in the conversation," Kikuchi-san said, taking pity on him. The slime hopped up and down like he was agreeing with her.

"I wanna be part of the party, too! Pigii!"

"Hey, you just talked in human language!"

"So Takei ended up as a monster...," Mimimi mused, sounding confused. I looked at poor Takei and considered the game.

"Interesting. So not everyone gets to play an adventurer."

"I suddenly became a fairy, so I bet it was the same for Takei."

"Yikes. Becoming slime is a horrible fate," I said, laughing wryly.

"Wh-what should we do? He's a monster, but he's still Takei?" Mimimi asked in a panic.

"You're right… I think we should take him down at once!" Kikuchi-san said decisively.

"I didn't know you were such a hawk! Maybe we can make friends with him!" Mimimi shouted in surprise. I was surprised, too.

"Yeah…he might be a trash mob, but he *is* Takei."

"Yeah, don't forget that!" slime-Takei jumped in.

"He's talking just like us!"

Mimimi was obviously thrown off by the flood of events. In real life, she can handle anything, but that didn't seem to be the case in this game.

"Grrr!!" the slime with Takei's voice said, hurling himself at me. *You'll pay for this, Takei!*

"Oof!"

"Brain!!"

"A-are you all right?!"

I stepped back, rubbing the spot where he'd hit me. But…what the heck was I feeling?

"Yeah. It doesn't hurt…but my head feels sort of heavy or something…"

"Your head feels heavy?"

"Um…I think it's because your PH fell!"

"You mean that's what it feels like to lose HP?"

"Oh right, HP…"

"This game is really well designed!"

"Pigiiiii!!"

While we were talking, slime-Takei had rapidly puffed up and started howling again. Dude, shut up.

"Eee! He's getting angry again because we're leaving him out!"

"Pigipigipigipigi!"

Hopping forward at lightning speed, he hurled himself at us again and again. This was getting ridiculous.

"He just attacked us like four times in a row!"

"He has multi-attacks?"

"He's stronger than I thought!"

"I know, this is one hell of a high-level slime…"

Mimimi and I jumped back a few feet, but slime-Takei hopped toward us again.

"…No, I don't think that was multi-attacks, just four hits in a row!"

"What a meathead…"

I slumped, disappointed, but Kikuchi-san refused to let us ease up.

"Nevertheless, he's still a threat. If you two don't do something, you'll lose the game!"

"As a gamer, I can't let myself lose to slime…"

"As a human, I can't let myself lose to Takei…"

Reacting to Mimimi's comment, the slime began boiling underneath its skin so that round welts bubbled up all over it.

"Pigiiiii!!!"

"Nanami-san, I don't think it would be wise to provoke Takei-kun any further!" Kikuchi-san warned.

Just then, light began to concentrate in the slime's body with a keening sound. What was happening?

"Oh no! I think he's getting ready to do something bad!" Mimimi shouted.

"It's a powerful spell used by slimes… If this plays out according to theory, it'll be one of the most powerful spells out there!"

"An endgame spell?! In the tutorial?!"

"This is bad! You've got to take him down while he's preparing!" Kikuchi-san shouted frantically.

Mimimi glanced around like she didn't know what to do. "But how?!"

"Nanami-san, use the knife in your belt! Tomozaki-kun, use the sword in your back holster!"

I drew the sword. "This? O-okay, got it!"

"I don't think he can defend himself right now!"

"Pigi?! Pigii…pigii…"

The slime must have seen where the situation was headed, because the tone of its voice changed.

"I th-think he's getting weaker..."

"Pigi...pigi... I'm scared..."

A look of pity gradually came over Mimimi's face.

"I feel so g-guilty..."

"I kn-know," Kikuchi-san agreed.

But I'm more used to gaming than either of them, and I kept my cool.

"Remember...it was Takei who attacked us just now."

"That's true..."

"I'm sorry, but this is for the sake of world peace! I'm gonna do it! Yaaa!" I thrust my sword straight into the slime.

"Pig...pigi..."

Its voice faded, and the slime vanished. *Sorry, Takei.*

"Takei is gone...," Mimimi whispered sorrowfully.

"I—I think it was the right decision... Maybe," Kikuchi-san said.

"What's with this lingering guilt after the battle?" I asked, frowning. I didn't get why we had to feel so bad about Takei.

"Eee!"

"Whoa!"

Just then, Mimimi and I shouted at the same moment.

"Wh-what's the matter?" Kikuchi-san asked.

"I j-just...," I began, looking down with trepidation at my body, "...felt something kind of ticklish..."

"Oh, I think that's called... Wait just a moment, all right? Here goes!"

Kikuchi-san stretched out both hands in front of her and prayed fervently. A book about the size of her body appeared.

"Something just materialized!"

"What's in that book?"

"It's the rule book...or at least, that's what I call it. It's got detailed information about various parts of the game."

Using both hands, she struggled to flip through the book floating in the air before her. So precious.

"...Oh, here it is. A level-up!"

I thought about what had just happened. "So leveling up tickles?"

"Yes. And it looks as if you kind of wish for it, a screen will appear... and you can check it there."

"Kind of wish for it...? Like this? Ta-daa!" Mimimi said. A blue, board-looking thing appeared in her hands.

"Wow! It's like a tablet!"

The three of us stared at it. There was a list of words like "Item," "Status," "Save," and "Options." Which meant...

"...This must be the menu screen in RPGs. We can see our status and items and other stuff."

"And there's a map!"

"Yes, that's right. Um, according to the rule book...the other players are playing their own roles in other parts of this world. Just like you two are a warrior and a thief, I'm the explanation fairy, and Takei is in the 'other' category."

"The 'other' category?" I echoed pityingly. At the same time, I couldn't help thinking it was perfect for him.

"So should we go look for everyone else?" Mimimi suggested.

"Yeah, that sounds like a good goal to start with," I answered. "How about we head for this port? It looks nearby on the map."

"I think that's an excellent plan!" Kikuchi-san said.

"Okay! Let's go!" I said, and Mimimi chimed in with a "Yeah!"

She started walking, looking at the map as she led the way.

"Follow me, noble adventurers!"

"...Uh, Mimimi? It's that way."

"It is?"

Turns out her sense of direction in the game was just as bad as in real life.

* * *

We moved forward following the map and eventually reached our destination.

"Well, here's the town... It's so quiet...," Mimimi said.

"And so pretty and clean," Kikuchi-san added.

We looked around. The atmosphere was subdued, with rows of similar-looking buildings. I thought about the standard risks in games like this. We seemed fairly safe for the moment.

"Yeah, nothing fancy, but I don't see a single piece of litter," I said.

"So that must mean it's safe? Hey, is that Tama?" Mimimi asked.

"Voices really carry far in a quiet place like this…," I said. Just then, a man walked out of an alley toward us.

"Oh, there's someone else."

"Hello!" the man said smoothly. "Welcome to Shuberg!"

That voice and expression were awfully familiar…

"Is that you, Mizusawa?" I asked. The man tilted his head, confused—but he was the spitting image.

"Mizusawa? What exotic Eastern name is that? I am Bell, mayor of this town!"

"He looks and sounds just like Takahiro to me," Mimimi said.

"It's definitely Mizusawa-kun," Kikuchi-san agreed.

"Come now, a mere chance resemblance. Pay that no mind, Mimimi."

"You just used my name!"

"Mizusawa sure is putting the RP in RPG," I said.

"Forget about that. Just listen to what I have to tell you."

"Fine," I said, nodding reluctantly as Mizusawa, aka Bell, grasped control of the situation.

"So…what did you want to tell us?" Mimimi asked, switching gears.

"Welcome once again to the town of Shuberg! We open our arms to adventurers! Please relax and enjoy your time here!"

"That sounded super scripted…but hey, at least we're welcome here!" Mimimi said happily.

"We didn't have anywhere to stay, so this could be perfect," I added.

"Yes, you'll be able to recover from your recent battle," Kikuchi-san said.

"Right?"

"All right, we'll take you up on that offer!" I said to Bell.

"Then follow me. Fumiya and Kikuchi-san, watch your step."

"He's literally Mizusawa."

"Definitely."

* * *

"Make yourselves at home in here," Bell-slash-Mizusawa said when we reached the large room in the inn that he'd led us to. I looked around in surprise.

"This place is huge, and there's six beds...um, Mizusawa?"

"The name is Bell."

"Okay, Bell-san. There are three of us...well, two people and one fairy. You don't need to give us so much space. Also, we don't have any money."

"Ha-ha, no need to worry. You don't need money around here. Please just take it easy."

"B-but I feel bad—," I started to say, when I was interrupted by ecstatic voices.

"Braiiin!! This bed is so soft! Wheee!"

"Look, Tomozaki-kun—there's a bed just my size! It's so warm...!"

Oblivious to my polite hesitation, the two of them were fully enjoying their beds. Oy.

"...Never mind. Thank you."

"Ha-ha-ha! You're most welcome."

Just as we were wrapping up our conversation, a knock came on the door.

"Ah, I believe your meal is ready!" Bell said to my surprise.

"You're feeding us, too?!"

Kikuchi-san and Mimimi leaped up from their beds to thank Bell.

"Th-thank you so much!"

"Count on Takahiro to do it right!"

"It's Bell, not Takahiro. All right, enjoy your rest," Bell said, slipping out as the food was brought in. From beginning to end, he was 100 percent Mizusawa.

"Well, he was really into that," I said.

"Yes, I think he's enjoying himself," Kikuchi-san added.

"Oooh, this looks like a feast! Steak, salad, even soup!"

"It does!" I said. "But I wonder...what will happen when we eat it? Does taste exist in VR?"

"Yes, I wonder... Oh! There's one in my size, too!"

"They think of everything in this game... Let's eat!"

"My thoughts exactly! Let's eat!" Mimimi said.

"Let's eat!" Kikuchi-san and I chimed in, diving into our meal.

"It's not so much tasty as..."

"It's like...a pleasant feeling, isn't it?" Kikuchi-san said.

"Yeah, almost a ticklish feeling, but not in a bad way... A little like when we got the level-up earlier."

"You're right!" I agreed.

"Is that how it felt?" Kikuchi-san asked.

I nodded.

"Yeah, I think it's the same feeling...which must mean everything positive, like leveling up or recovery, feels like this."

"Oh, I get it! That's what I imagined a VR game would be like!"

"How strange... Eating is ticklish now..."

I was getting excited, even though I didn't understand how the overall system was set up. "Yeah, this game is amazing... I wonder what's coming next."

"Ah-ha-ha. Makes your gamer's heart skip a beat, huh?"

"Something like that. I'm itching to try everything out."

"Well, should we finish off this meal and then go to sleep so we're rested for tomorrow?" Kikuchi-san proposed.

"You mean recover? I'm all for it!"

As we got ready for bed, I thought about the scenario.

"Sleep, huh? I wonder how time works in this game."

"Oh well...according to the rule book, everyone in the party gets under their covers and closes their eyes for a few seconds, and then it's morning and they're fully recovered."

"Ah-ha-ha, sounds like an RPG," I said.

"What?! I wanted to sleep in this fluffy bed for hours!"

"No way! That'd be a waste of a good adventure!"

"Tee-hee. You're enjoying this, aren't you, Tomozaki-kun!"

With that, all three of us lay down on our pillowy beds.

* * *

And then it was morning.

"Good morning!!" Mimimi shouted.

"Wow, you're perky. Didn't you say you wanted to sleep for hours?"

"I know how you feel," Kikuchi-san said. "I only closed my eyes for a few seconds, but somehow I feel so refreshed."

"Yeah, I know… I guess this must mean our recovery is complete?"

"Could be! Okay! Let's get this adventure started again!"

"Tee-hee. You're so full of energy, Nanami-san."

With our strength back, it was time to head to our next destination—which was a problem.

"…We don't know where anyone else is, and we don't even know our objectives." I was starting to feel lost.

"Well, according to the rule book…the goal seems to be to rescue the world from the control of an evil demon."

"Sounds like a beta version of a beta version to me…"

"Well, it is a demo, so it seems they've simplified it quite a bit…"

"So for now, we focus on killing the evil demon? Got it! Leave it to Minami Nanami! I've got this!"

She was about to race out of the room, but I stopped her.

"Wait, wait! This may be a demo version, but our level is still too low to face the final boss, and our party is too small!"

"It is?"

"At the very least, we need someone who can use offensive magic and someone who can heal."

"You can't, Brain? When I looked at the 'Status' category or whatever, I think there was something about MP. So that must mean magic points?"

"I'm a warrior…so I should be able to use it, but my level is low… I think we'd be better off with someone who specializes in that."

"So you'll start by searching for the others after all?" Kikuchi-san asked.

"Yeah. But first of all, let's get out of here."

"Got it!"

* * *

As we left the inn, Bell-slash-Mizusawa came out to see us off.

"Beautiful morning, isn't it? Well, everyone, best of luck in the battle," he said and vanished into the building. We hadn't paid him a cent.

"…He really did give us everything for free," Mimimi said, sounding conscience-stricken.

"Yes…" Kikuchi-san nodded.

"He said the town welcomes adventurers, but I wonder why he did all that for us."

I thought about it for a minute, but I couldn't come up with a good answer. Hmm.

"Well, it's Takahiro we're talking about. I can't help thinking he had some ulterior motive," Mimimi said. "He even gave us all weapons and armor and recovery items, and then he told us how to get to the next town."

"I doubt he decided to do all that on his own… Maybe since this is a demo version and this is the first town, they made it easy for training purposes?"

"You mean, it doesn't have to do with the story itself?"

"Yeah. But given how high the quality is, it seems like there'd be some other reason for him to be kind to adventurers—some reason related to the plot."

I thought back on other games I'd played, searching for an answer.

"Maybe, but this town is so quiet, and everyone looks so happy… I don't feel like any crisis is going on here."

"I know…"

"But what do you think that means?"

"...As far as I can figure out...," I began, having hit on an idea. Mimimi looked at me curiously. "He gave us a place to stay and equipment and items, so we don't need to stop at shops for any of those things. And he told us the way to the next town, so we don't have to ask the townspeople for information... Which makes me think..."

"Oh, I see," Kikuchi-san said, figuring it out herself.

"Wait, what? Tell me!" Mimimi said.

"If you think about it...what if Mizusawa—I mean, Bell—doesn't want us to talk to anyone else in town?"

"...What?" Mimimi asked, sounding confused.

"What he means is...Bell is trying to prevent us from finding something hidden here," Kikuchi-san explained.

I nodded.

"Oh, that makes sense," Mimimi said. "If we get our information and items from him, we won't need to talk to anyone else, and we can head straight to the next town."

"...Which means that if we poke around here, we might discover something," I said.

Mimimi suddenly looked excited. "Maybe we'll find everyone else!"

"That's a possibility."

Kikuchi-san smiled, too, like she was getting more interested in playing.

"Well then...shall we stay here and look around?"

"Yeah, sounds like a plan," I said, and we set off to explore.

* * *

After a little while, we spotted a townsperson walking down the street.

"Excuse me!" I called.

"Yes?" the townsperson answered casually.

"...Is this guy Takei, too?" I muttered, but the townsperson just tilted his head.

"Takei? Who's that?"

"His voice sounds different," Kikuchi-san said.

"I guess there are NPCs, too."

"NCPs...?" Kikuchi-san echoed.

The townsperson scowled angrily at us. "I'd appreciate it if you don't confuse me with Takei."

"Oh, wait, I think this is Mizusawa," I said, almost certain I was right.

"He loves acting, doesn't he!" Mimimi agreed.

"If it's Mizusawa, I bet he's a bad guy."

"You're not being very kind to Mizusawa-kun..."

Ignoring our conversation, the townsperson addressed all three of us. "Are you adventurers?"

"Um, yes, we are. Takahiro...I mean, *good sir*, do adventurers come to this town often?" Mimimi asked.

"Oh, yes," he began fluently. "I'd say they come through about once a week. But Master Bell takes care of them all, so they're soon on their way to the next town."

"As I suspected," I muttered.

"Yes, and that's why we're always on schedule."

"On schedule?"

"What, you don't know about the Schedule? Well, that explains why you look so lost. I understand now."

I sure didn't. I frowned, as lost as Mimimi.

"Wh-what do you mean?"

"Are you interested...in the essence of happiness?" the townsperson said.

"Um, uh...," Mimimi said in a fluster.

"Oh, I'm very sorry. It's almost sundown, and today at sundown, I'm supposed to discover a girl in town causing mischief. I'd best be going."

"What? Oh, um, you are?" Mimimi said.

"Good-bye, then. Thanks be to Master Bell and the happiness promised to us."

Just as the townsperson was about to leave, a youthful voice called to us.

"Guys!!"

We turned around.

"Tama?!"

"Hey, it's Tama-chan!"

"Natsubayashi-san, you're here, too!"

Meanwhile, the townsperson's expression turned severe. "What have we here? Young Hanabi, you're not following the Schedule. It seems you intend to betray us after all."

"Oh…no…," she said, backing away fearfully.

"And these must be your fellow traitors?"

"Wh-what are you talking about?"

Mimimi looked back and forth between Tama-chan and the townsperson, waiting to see what would happen.

"Death to the traitors!"

"D-death?"

"This is getting ugly!"

Mimimi and I exchanged glances.

"A situation like this…calls for smoke!" Tama hurled some sort of energy at the ground. Sand flew up, instantly blocking my vision.

"Wow! A huge dust cloud!"

"Come on, guys, this way!" she yelled, leading the three of us to the road under the cover of the swirling dust.

* * *

Once we were safely in a back alley, we shared another round of greetings.

"I'm so glad I found you guys! Mimimi and Tomozaki and…Fuka-chan, you look kind of small!"

"It seems…I'm a fairy in this game."

"I love it! It's perfect for you!" Tama-chan said, which made Kikuchi-san smile and blush. As always, Tama-chan said exactly what she was thinking. She grinned.

"I bet you're glad there's finally someone smaller than you!" Mimimi teased.

"Shut up and mind your own business!" Tama-chan snapped back. This felt just like real life.

"Anyway, what are you wearing, Tama? Some kind of green martial arts outfit with a red scarf? Whew, breaking the mold! So cute!"

"Um, I'm the daughter of a martial arts family that runs a karate dojo outside this town!"

"...That outfit does look like something a monk would wear," I said, thinking back to similar characters I'd seen in RPGs. She had on a green Chinese-style dress with an orange scarf, and her hair was tied in pigtails.

"So you do karate...so you must have a strong heart and strong body... but you're still small...how cute! Starting today, I'm Team Tama!"

"Uh, I think you've supported her all along...," I remarked as Mimimi spun out of control. She stuck her tongue out at me.

"...We have more important things to do than argue!" Tama-chan reminded us.

"You're right. What on earth just happened?" Kikuchi-san asked.

"...Well, this town is a little bit strange...," Tama-chan began slowly.

*   *   *

"Oh, so that's what the townsperson meant when he said that," I said. Everything made sense now.

"So Takahiro...I mean, Bell...controls the actions of everyone in this town?" Mimimi said, thinking as she talked.

"Yes, everyone receives a schedule, and you have to do what it says. It tells you where to go, what to do, who to be friends with, and who to marry. He says if you follow the Schedule, you'll be happy."

"Happy?" Kikuchi-san muttered, frowning.

"Mayor Bell used to be an excellent fortune-teller...and I've heard that if you do what he says, you do meet good people and find good work and live a good life, but..."

"You can't do what you want?" I asked. The town policy sounded to me like the polar opposite of Tama-chan's own approach to life.

"So free will has no place here?" Kikuchi-san asked.

Tama-chan nodded.

"Yes, it's like a dystopia. My mom and dad in this world met thanks to the Schedule, and they say they're grateful to him for that, but this life feels too rigid to me—"

"Ah-ha-ha! Yeah, I could never see you going along with that!" Mimimi interrupted.

"No. And…"

Just then, I heard someone shouting from the end of the alley.

"There they are! Over there!"

I had a bad feeling about this. I turned around and saw a soldier in armor pointing at us.

"…So that means…"

"When I said I didn't want to follow the Schedule, he treated me like a traitor!"

"I knew it!"

My suspicions were correct. The next instant, we found ourselves in the dead end of an alley.

"You're trapped! You'll never escape now!"

"They found us! Looks like we'll have to fight!" Mimimi shouted excitedly, obviously enjoying the game now.

"Be careful! He's way stronger than that slime you fought before!" Kikuchi-san warned.

"Got it! Leave it to Mimimi-chan!"

"Mimimi, you're a thief. You're supposed to play support."

"I am?"

"It's okay! I'm a martial artist, so I can fight!"

"Tama-chan and I will be the front guard while you distract him, Mimimi! Here we go!"

"Hmm, this isn't quite what I imagined," Mimimi mumbled, scratching her cheek. Meanwhile, Tama-chan and I started fighting the soldier.

* * *

The open field we were in turned into a box, like the shift to a battle map in a game. Apparently, we weren't going to be able to run away from this fight.

"So you wanna fight, traitors? The, uh, wraith of Master Bell shall…fall on you!" the soldier said incoherently. Once again, the voice sounded a lot like Takei's.

"Wraith?" I echoed, confused. After a brief silence, Mimimi lit up.

"...Do you mean...wrath?"

"Oh, yes, *wrath* and *wraith* look very similar," Kikuchi-san said, nodding. The soldier pointed at the two of them happily.

"Yeah, that's what it was! Wrath!"

I sighed. "You seem awfully relaxed for a battle, Takei..."

"Dude, shut up!"

The moment the soldier-slash-Takei lost his cool, Mimimi pounced. "I'm gonna get you!" She pulled the knife from her belt and lunged at the solider. But...

"Ha! Doesn't work, does it?"

"My knife bounced off him!"

Her attack failed.

"His armor must defend against physical attacks! This sucks—none of us can use magic!"

While we panicked, the soldier shouted, "Charge!" in Takei's voice and raised his greatsword to bring it down on Mimimi.

"Mimimi, watch out!"

"Brain!!"

I leaped in front of her, taking the soldier's attack.

"Oof!"

"Tomozaki-kun, are you all right?!" Kikuchi-san asked.

"Brain, I'm s-sorry you had to shield me..."

"It's fine. I probably have the highest defense of anyone in this party... Can I have a potion, though?"

"B-Brain... Okay, here it is!" Mimimi said, selecting an item from the menu and giving it to me.

"Thanks. I feel better... But I wonder how we can inflict damage on him..."

Suddenly, Tama-chan, who until now had been watching from the sidelines, turned toward the soldier.

"...I'm gonna try something!" She crouched down, then dashed toward him. "Open hand strike!"

Her strike from below caught his chin and sent his helmet flying up.

"I feel dizzy!"

Kikuchi-san watched in surprise. "He's staggering!"

"I thought I'd rattle his head a little!" Tama-chan said cheerfully.

Mimimi looked unsettled. "Wait, so you're actually good at martial arts, Tama?"

"Not really, but as I was looking at his armor, the idea just kind of hit me..."

"Oh, interesting...so this must be one of those RPGs where skills come to you in a flash while you're fighting... Hey, Mimimi!"

"What?"

"Will you stare at that soldier for a minute and see if any ideas hit you?"

"Stare at him...? Oh!"

"Did a light bulb go on?"

"Heh-heh-heh. Leave it to Mimimi!"

Our resident sprinter started running—and in an instant, she was at the soldier's side.

"You're so fast!"

"Piece of cake!"

With a sound like a key turning in a lock, the soldier's armor fell apart and clattered to the ground. He was completely vulnerable.

"How's that for a guard break?"

"His armor is off!"

"The rest is up to you, Brain!"

"Okay! Ahhhhh!"

I dashed forward and thrust my warrior's sword through the soldier. Physically speaking, I didn't actually slice him in two, but the sense of resistance lingered in my arm.

"Aaaaargh! You got me, didn't you?!" the soldier screamed in Takei's voice, crumpling to the ground.

"Yes! He's down!"

"You did it!"

While Mimimi and Kikuchi-san shouted happily, Tama-chan gazed at the motionless body of the soldier.

"...Poor Takei," she said softly.

"That goes for real life, too," I answered. Just then, that familiar pleasant feeling coursed through my body. Several times in a row, in fact.

"Does that mean...I just leveled up multiple times?"

"It's shaking all through me!" Tama-chan said, sounding surprised. For some reason, Mimimi was writhing around.

"I could get addicted to this!"

"Definitely!"

Suddenly, the fallen soldier reached his left hand up toward the sky.

"M-M-Master Bell, may you perspire!!"

With that, his arm flopped down by his side. Tama-chan crept timidly up and peered at him.

"He's not moving anymore."

"Yeah," I said, nodding.

"Those were pretty weird last words," Mimimi said, as if she'd just realized something. "I bet that in the script it was supposed to be 'prosper,' not 'perspire'..."

Yup, he'd done it again.

"Oh, he misread the script?" Kikuchi-san said awkwardly.

"Well, it's not his fault—he's Takei after all," I said, trying to make her feel better. About what, I'm not sure.

"...Yeah. But forget about that, we've gotta get out of here!" Mimimi shouted, coming back to her senses.

"You're right. If we stay here, more soldiers will probably find us. And they seem to be the type who crack down on traitors mercilessly...," I said, coolly analyzing the situation.

"Y-yes, but...," Tama-chan said anxiously. Mimimi thumped her on the shoulder.

"We can talk later! For now, let's run until we feel safe!"

"O-okay!"

We all started running toward the end of the alleyway.

* * *

We ran around town trying to find somewhere safe, but every time a townsperson spotted us, they made a big fuss and blocked our way.

"Shit! Wherever we go, the townspeople recognize us!" I said, leading the pack.

"I bet an emergency change was posted in everyone's Schedule... He's able to change them in real time using magic...," Tama-chan answered, looking panicked.

"Then we'll have to leave town, won't we?" Kikuchi-san asked.

"The gates leading out of town are probably all shut! We'll have to find a secret passage...," Tama-chan said anxiously, looking around.

"I wish there was someone who could save us!" Mimimi shouted.

Tama-chan's head snapped up, as if an idea had just hit her.

"...This way!"

"Did you think of something?!"

"Yeah, the place where I've been hiding! My family has been protecting me! I don't know if we can all fit, but just make sure no one is following you!"

Mimimi grinned. "Got it! When I leveled up, I got a stealth skill, so I'll use that!"

"Nice! Figures, since you're a thief!"

"Leave it to me! It'll affect all of you!"

With that, the four of us started sneaking through the alleyways.

* * *

"Tiptoe, tiptoe... Are we there yet?"

Mimimi's feet were sparkling as she recited an incantation that I suspect wasn't actually necessary. I think the sparkles mean she was using the stealth skill.

"Yup, we're here."

"This...is where you've been hiding?" I asked.

"Is it a storehouse?" Kikuchi-san said.

We were looking at an old wooden building that definitely didn't seem like a place people lived.

"It's the shed from a toolmaker's shop that got knocked down. I've been hiding here because there was a lot of nonperishable food stored here. For now, it's safe because everyone is so busy following the Schedule they've forgotten all about this place."

"They have?" Mimimi asked worriedly. All the same, we decided to crowd in.

"My dad and big sister are in there right now...and my mom must be out getting water."

"Hello... Hey, it's Yuzu!" Mimimi blurted out when her eyes met Izumi's inside the shed.

"You're all here?!"

She scanned our party. I was equally surprised to see her.

"Wh-what are you doing here?"

"Oh, I forgot to tell you. She's my sister," Tama-chan said, like that was entirely natural.

"Your sister...?"

Mimimi seemed disturbed by this bombshell.

"Yes, Hanabi-chan is my little sister!" Izumi said.

"Sh-she is...? My cute, adorable little Tama...is Yuzu's little sister... umm..."

"You seem very shaken by that," I said. I was concerned, but I wanted to see what emotion she would ultimately land on.

"—I can accept that!" she finally said.

"Glad to hear it," I said with a relieved but not surprised sigh.

"Uh, 'scuse me," a man who appeared to be Tama-chan's dad said, coughing. I knew immediately who it was.

"It's Takei."

"Definitely Takei," Kikuchi-san agreed. We exchanged glances and sniggered.

"Who are you guys?" he asked.

"Oh, I'm sorry. You must be Izumi's dad, right?" Mimimi asked.

He grinned cheerfully. "Bingo!"

"Definitely Takei."

"Definitely."

Kikuchi-san and I exchanged another glance.

"We're friends of Tama and Yuzu!"

"Oh, you're my daughter's friends? Well then, make yourselves at home!" he said, pointing in the air. As Takei likes to do.

"He seems very relaxed," Kikuchi-san said.

"Kind of undignified for a dad…"

Just then, I heard the sounds of metal clashing and fists hitting flesh, like a fight was going on

"Uh-oh, what's happening?" the concerned father asked in Takei's voice.

"It sounds like…M-Mom!" Izumi yelped.

"Oh no!" Tama-chan said in shock.

We all burst outside.

"Look!"

"Hoofprints, signs of a fight…and blood," Kikuchi-san said. The prints were fresh.

"It can't be!" Izumi was freaking out now. Something was clearly very wrong—but neither their mother nor the soldier was anywhere to be found.

"Do you think she was…kidnapped?" Mimimi asked.

"Based on the evidence, yes… And her life could be at risk," I said.

The face of Izumi's-father-slash-Takei clouded over with an expression of despair so profound I could hardly believe it was Takei.

"But…no soldier following the Schedule should have found us here…"

Tama-chan looked even more stricken.

"It's all my fault…"

"Hanabi-chan?"

"I did something I shouldn't have, like I always do…and that's why the Schedule was updated…" Tama-chan's voice gradually trailed off.

"M-maybe, but it's only a game!"

"Yeah! It's only a game, so you don't have to feel bad!"

Tama-chan was not reassured by Mimimi and Izumi's attempts.

"But…if the game is this realistic, it's no different from interacting with real people."

"You really think so?" Izumi asked. I could tell she didn't agree, but she was trying to be understanding.

"If that's how she feels, who are we to argue?" Mimimi said, nodding.

"We have to save her!" Tama-chan said, looking up with a determined glint in her eye. "We have to save our mother!"

"Hanabi-chan…," Kikuchi-san said, startled. But I understood her line of thinking.

"…You're right," I said forcefully.

"B-Brain?"

"I know this is a game; it's not real. It's technically okay if someone dies here."

"Right," Izumi said, nodding.

"But…I'm not going to be lazy because of that. I always try hardest when I'm playing video games. I think…that's what it means to be a gamer," I said.

Kikuchi-san giggled. "You're right," she said. I was surprised but happy to have her support. "I feel the same way. I ended up in this role by chance, but now that I've got it, I think it's more fun to give it my all."

"Thanks. I know I'm a pain in the butt," Tama-chan said, sounding a little depressed.

Mimimi thumped her on the shoulder. "No, you're not! Well, maybe kinda, but that's why I like you!" she said.

"It is? Thanks." Tama-chan glanced away, blushing slightly.

"Okay then, let's act like this is real life, and we're going to save their mother! If there's a chance she's still alive, we've got to do everything we can to rescue her!" I said, leading the party in true warrior fashion. I can do this kind of stuff in a game, at least.

"R-really? If that's what you all want to do, then I'm in," Izumi said. She didn't seem fully convinced, but she was kind enough to go along with the plan.

"Launch Operation Rescue Mom!" Mimimi announced.

"By the way, what's your job, Izumi-san?" Kikuchi-san asked, glancing at her as if she'd suddenly realized something.

"My job?"

Izumi isn't much of a gamer, so I explained.

"Like, are you a magician or a warrior or what?"

"Oh, that? It said I'm a white mage or something."

"Ooh! So you know about recovery!"

"Yes! I can use recovery magic!"

I nodded happily at her. She was exactly the sort of person we'd been looking for. Mimimi smiled, too.

"That's perfect! We were just saying we needed someone who could help us with that!"

"I think we've got enough people in our party now! A warrior, a monk, a thief, and a white mage. Not a bad mix!"

"Awesome! Then let's go!" Mimimi said, and the rest of the group shouted their agreement.

"Wait, first let's go kill some random soldiers outside of town so we can level up," I said.

"You're so rational, Brain."

* * *

We were standing in front of Bell's mansion.

"So we're finally here...," Mimimi said, craning her neck up to look at the huge building.

We were squarely in enemy territory. If we let our guard down for a second, we'd be dead meat.

"At least your level is much higher now," Kikuchi-san said. Everyone nodded. Once we started killing soldiers, we got addicted to the level-up buzz, so I'm pretty sure we were all plenty strong now. Whether that was enough to take down the boss was another question.

"So this is Mizusawa's mansion...," I mumbled nervously.

"His name is Bell, so maybe you should call him that?" Tama-chan said.

"Nah, it's annoying," I answered as bluntly as her.

"Did you hear that, Kikuchi-san?"

"Um, yes...," she said, shrinking back from our brutally honest exchange. *Ack, sorry!*

"Well, what should we do? We could walk straight in the front door like we owned the place...but usually if you do that in these situations, you fall into a trap," I said, thinking out loud. Mimimi pointed to the back of the mansion.

"In that case...let's go this way!"

"Do you know something we don't?" Izumi asked, tilting her head.

Mimimi stuck her finger in the air proudly. "No, but when I leveled up, I got a lock-picking skill, so I think I can get us in the back door!"

"Wow, you're a great crook!" Izumi said enthusiastically, but since she doesn't really understand gaming, I think she was just playing along. Mimimi wagged her finger.

"I'm a thief, okay? Crook doesn't sound very good."

"Thief, crook, whatever! Let's just go," Tama-chan said, efficiently slicing the Gordian knot.

Meanwhile, I was gloating to myself. "Heh-heh, looks like those level-ups have worked!"

"Brain, that smile is creepy..."

"Let's see—where's the door...," Izumi said, looking around. "Ah, right here!"

"I think it's what we're looking for," Kikuchi-san agreed.

"Good. Let's get in there!" I said, and we stepped into the mansion.

* * *

Meanwhile, on the second floor...

"I believe they've entered the building."

"Indeed. Takahiro, can you do something about it?"

A woman was sitting on a throne with a stylish male attendant beside her in the dimly lit room. They seemed to be enjoying themselves.

"...I told you to call me Bell here."

"Did you? In that case, you'll need to speak to me more respectfully."

"Fine, fine, Your Highness."

"That's better."

"Anyway, want me to go down first?"

"…'Want me to'?"

"Oh right—would you prefer if I go down first, Your Highness?"

"Hee-hee, yes, please do that, Takahiro."

"I told you… Oh, never mind. As you wish."

* * *

"Looks like the first floor is clear. I'm searching with my thief senses, but I don't detect anyone."

"Thieves sure come in handy," I joked, but I was impressed by the way she was putting her abilities to maximum use.

"I think…there are people in the basement and on the second floor!"

"Then that must mean there's a dungeon in the basement and Bell is on the second floor," Kikuchi-san said.

"Seems likely. Dungeons in RPGs are always down…which means…!"

When I said that, Tama-chan's face suddenly brightened.

"She's alive!"

"We don't know that yet. The people down there could be guards," I reminded them.

Tama-chan nodded. "…You're right. Let's get going!"

The five of us headed down.

"Over there!" Kikuchi-san was pointing at a female figure.

"A woman in the dungeon… That must mean…!"

Mimimi finished my sentence for me. "It must be their mother!"

I nodded. I figured we were about to witness an emotional family reunion, but…

"…Yuzucchi! Tama!!"

Their mother started talking in Takei's voice.

"Hey, why does their mom sound like Takei, too?!" I shouted. How was that allowed? They better patch that.

"I'm having a hard time feeling emotional about this...," Mimimi said, smiling wryly. I didn't know how to react, either.

"It's amazing that Hanabi-chan took this seriously and genuinely tried to save her..."

"Why? I mean, if he's supposed to be my mom, then he's my mom!" Tama-chan said, as if that made any sense. Izumi turned to us with a pleading look.

"Okay, now you guys understand why I couldn't empathize, right?!"

"Yes, I do now...," Kikuchi-san said.

"I can see how that would be ha—," I started to say, when I heard the door open.

"The game is up."

"...That sounds like Mizusa... I mean, Bell," I said.

Bell sighed. "If only you'd gone to the next town like I told you...but no, you had to go and poke your noses where they didn't belong."

"Shut up and give us back our mother!" Tama-chan cried with an impressive level of drama. She's amazing.

"That's an impossible request," Mizusawa answered, matching her.

Izumi and Mimimi watched them and whispered to each other.

"Hiro's really into this!"

"Yuzu, you can't say things like that in the middle of the game!"

But Izumi was right—Mizusawa had clearly been enjoying this all along.

"Don't chat among yourselves; I'm talking!" he scolded sharply.

"Yessir!" Izumi answered, straightening her posture.

"But why did you kidnap their mother?!" I asked, getting into my role for the moment.

"She was getting in the way of the ideal community I am creating here. It's as simple as that," he said in a leisurely tone.

"'Ideal community'...?" Kikuchi-san echoed.

"I have the power to divine the perfect, ideal state of the world. I construct the scenarios that the gods communicate to me, and if everything goes according to my plans, everyone in the world will be equal and happy. Needless to say, that includes both the human and demon races."

I could tell Tama-chan was getting angrier and angrier.

"But you ignore how everyone else feels!" she shouted emotionally. "Some of us have things we want to do!"

Mizusawa refused to budge.

"Yes, some people do. There is some truth to what you say, young lady. But more people do not. They find it's easier to simply do as they're told, and they're happier that way. You may want to walk your own path, but do you have the right to force others to do the same?"

"That's…"

"If you want to leave this town by yourself, be my guest. But if you try to brainwash your family and friends into leaving together, I won't stand for it. After all, your friends and family are an important part of my community. What's wrong with that?"

"…!"

"Tama…"

His speech left her wordless.

"Just like you don't want to be condemned for forging ahead, other people want their weak way of life affirmed. In this town, we offer those weak people their promised happiness."

"Wh-when you put it like that…," Kikuchi-san said, sounding half convinced.

"Your family was happy here. Innocently, unquestioningly happy. Until you began enticing them to leave. You, Hanabi, are the one who destroyed that for them."

"You think…I…"

Just then, Izumi raised her head, no longer staring at the floor.

"…But!"

"Izumi?!"

"But our family matters to us!!"

Tama-chan stared at Izumi in a daze as she earnestly protested.

"…Yuzu-chan."

"You may be selfishly going after what you want…but is it really so bad to want the family members you love so much to be themselves instead of being part of some ideal 'community'?!"

"Why are you being so stubborn?"

"Hiro, you of all people should understand! You should admire people with a strong sense of self!"

"…I'm not Hiro. I'm Bell."

"That doesn't matter! Bell should understand, too!"

"…Damn it. Fine."

"Bell— I mean, Hiro…?"

"Geez, you sure are taking this seriously. But fine, you got me. I'm starting to reconsider my position."

Abruptly, the tension drained from Bell-slash-Mizusawa's body.

"Which means…"

"Whatever, it's fine. Who cares if Tama and her family go free? Four less people in this town won't make much of a difference anyway."

"…We convinced you?"

"Not exactly… Bell doesn't understand Izumi's point, but I do, so we can skip the fight."

"Takahiro! I knew there was some goodness in there somewhere!" Mimimi announced happily. Mizusawa let out a cold sigh.

"I suppose. Anyhow, you'd better get going before you're discov—"

That very moment, we heard the sound of hard heels tapping on the floor. Gradually, the sound came closer.

"Dear me, Bell. Aren't you being a bit too kind?" a voice said.

"Well, speak of the devil," Mizusawa answered, sighing with a wry smile. The clicking of footsteps grew louder until a form appeared in the doorway.

"Oh my, what a heartwarming scene."

"…Aoi?!"

There stood Aoi Hinami, dressed as an actual demon.

"Dear me, it will never do for a commoner to address me so casually. I am the Demon Queen. Demon Queen Aoi Hinami, that is."

"D-Demon Queen…?" Kikuchi-san echoed; even she was overwhelmed.

"So you've finally become a real final boss, eh?"

I, on the other hand, was impressed for a different reason altogether.

"Damn it, now I don't know what to tell you." Mizusawa sighed, raising one eyebrow. "You can try to escape, but you won't get far."

"Wh-what do we do? F-f-fight her?!" Izumi stuttered, clearly terrified.

"B-but her stats are unbelievably high!"

Mimimi was getting swept up in the panic, too. I mean, this version of Hinami really was overwhelming in her power.

"You're right. A party like you could never take me down… But I don't feel like fighting right now anyhow."

Tama-chan tilted her head in confusion.

"You don't?"

"I simply want to create a world where the demon race and the human race can live as equals."

Izumi stared into Hinami's eyes as if she were searching for the true meaning of her words.

"The demon race and the human race?"

Hinami nodded. "In today's world, the human race controls nearly everything. But my ideal is for us to live in harmony, each in their own place, with neither receiving preference over the other."

"That would be nice if it were possible…but it's probably not realistic," I argued.

"Um…I think the problem is…that demons eat humans, right?" Kikuchi-san added.

"Yes. But that's no different from humans eating livestock. That's why we of the demon race will promise to raise certain humans as livestock, and those will be the only ones we eat. We'll raise them in ranches just like this town."

That's when everything fell into place.

"Oh, I get it… So in the story, this town is a prototype for a livestock ranch where every aspect of people's lives is fully managed?"

"Stop talking about the 'story.'"

"Oh, sorry."

Hinami apparently took offense at my meta-analysis. For a moment, the group fell into an awkward silence. Hinami coughed, pulling herself together.

"…This is what I am proposing. The demon race and the human race will divide the living space equally between them, and the demons will raise humans as livestock to eat. In exchange, they will not interfere in the human communities. Needless to say, we will lodge no complaints about humans who raise animals as livestock. We don't even mind if you raise demons to eat. What do you say?"

"It does sound fair…"

"You're asking if we'll accept ranches like this town?"

Mimimi and Izumi both seemed unsure about which side to come down on.

"No way! We can't let them build human ranches!" Tama-chan exclaimed.

"But it's true that people raise pigs and cows to eat…," Kikuchi-san responded.

"Yes, I guess that's t-true…" Tama-chan was getting swayed by her words.

"Wh-what should we do?! Brain, what do you think?!"

"What?! Me?!"

"Yeah, tell us what to do, Tomozaki! I can't figure out hard stuff like this!" Mimimi went on. Izumi nodded. For some reason, everything now rested on my shoulders. Why???

"Y-you're kidding me…"

"If you're such a great gamer, you should be able to figure this out! It's in your hands!" Mimimi said.

"Yes! If Minmi says it's up to you, then I do, too!" Tama-chan piled on, looking straight at me. I wish she wouldn't do that at moments like this.

"Yeah, and you're a warrior, too," Mizusawa said. For me, that was the decisive argument.

"Well…you do have a point," I said. Warriors do tend to make the final decision at these critical moments. I couldn't deny that.

So I started analyzing the situation. Like Hinami said, the system she was proposing was fair. And if it could be maintained, it could probably lead to lasting peace… But…

"Nope, we can't accept it," I said confidently, having arrived at my conclusion.

"…Really now. And why is that?" Hinami asked.

"You're right that people eat pigs and cows, and that's generally accepted."

"As I said!" she interjected imposingly, then waited for me to continue.

"But doing the same with humans, raising them and eating them in the exact same way—that's unacceptable!"

"Tomozaki-kun…," Kikuchi-san said, her voice tinged with worry.

"You want inequality, not equality. Is that what you're saying?" Hinami asked.

"Of course! Because we're humans!"

"…Idiotic, egotistical creatures," Hinami said with a scornful frown. My determination did not waver. This was the answer of Tomozaki the Warrior, and it would not change.

"Okay, Brain! Understood!" Mimimi said cheerfully with a nod.

"Yes, I'll fight for that!" Tama-chan said, also nodding.

"And me too!" Izumi chimed in.

"Interesting. Because you're human, eh?" Mizusawa said, smiling pleasantly.

"…That is most unfortunate. Well, I'll do you the favor of ending your misery quickly," Hinami said.

"Damn it… She's so powerful… Obviously her level is way higher than mine…"

I felt myself being drawn in by her aura, but I gritted my teeth and held my ground.

"We made our decision, and we'll stick to it!" Mimimi announced, sounding positive despite Hinami's queenly presence.

"Mom, forgive me if I don't make it through this…!" Tama-chan stared at Hinami, clearly determined to see the fight to its end.

"If things turn bad, you guys run without me, okay? I can always heal!" Izumi said, apparently ready to fulfill her role as white mage.

That's when Kikuchi-san, our guiding fairy, spoke up.

"…Don't worry, everyone—you'll be fine! Um…according to the rule book, since this is a demo, the strength of the Demon Queen is low enough for us to easily take her down!"

"Wait, what?"

The Demon Queen herself was the first to let out a startled exclamation. After a slight lag, the rest of us registered what Kikuchi-san's words meant, too. And then...

"Yaaaaaaaa!"

The lopsided four-on-one harassment of Hinami began.

* * *

And that was how we trounced the Demon Queen Aoi Hinami, whose stats were in fact far lower than her appearance had led us to believe.

"D-damn it...looks like this is the end."

"That was easy." I grinned.

"I've still got lots of MP left!" Izumi said, also in excellent spirits.

"I wasn't even hitting her as hard as I could," Tama-chan said, unfazed by the fight.

"Aoi's so slow she didn't even manage to hit me once!" Mimimi said, smiling like she was really enjoying herself.

"I'm just watching 'cause I don't want to get hurt myself," Mizusawa said with a casual laugh as he gazed at Hinami.

"Those level-ups you all got outside of town seem to have paid off," Kikuchi-san noted.

"Actually, if you think about it, leveling up this high in a demo is kind of wrong," I said, but I was happy with the outcome. It wasn't often that I got to see Hinami lose. *Wonder if you can take screenshots in this game... I'd love to preserve this moment for posterity.*

"...I'm the type who likes to be surrounded by strong people, so starting today I'm on your side," Mizusawa said casually.

"Unbelievable! You're so self-serving!" Tama-chan scolded.

"*Gasp...* But remember this," Hinami said, staggering from her wounds. "You didn't win today because you were right...you're right because you won...!"

"Pretty words—but not very convincing coming from a weakling like her," Mizusawa said.

"Yeah. In RPGs, the balance is as important as the story," I added.

"What's happening...? It's too horrible...," Hinami cried, collapsing to the ground before falling silent.

"Hinami-san...farewell," Kikuchi-san said prayerfully, watching her depart the world. That was the signal for bouncy music to start blaring through the whole mansion.

"Ooh, this must be the ending!" said Mimimi.

"That was so fun! Let's play again after it goes on sale for real!"

Izumi may have had trouble empathizing with her fictional mother, but she genuinely seemed to have enjoyed the game.

"Yeah, I just wish we could save our data for next time," Mizusawa said, sounding satisfied.

"I know, but usually demo versions like this are separate from the real game."

"But it was fun!" Kikuchi-san laughed.

Tama-chan nodded happily. "I thought so, too!"

Hearing them say that made the gamer in me happy.

"Ha-ha. I'm glad even you two nongamers liked it."

From inside her dungeon cell, Mother shouted a happy "That was great!"

"I still can't get used to hearing someone who looks like a mom talk with Takei's voice," I said, smiling wryly.

Just then, we heard an echoey voice.

"Hey, don't you think it's strange that I'm the only one who's not there?"

"I hear someone calling from heaven!" Mizusawa joked.

"Ah-ha-ha! Awww, poor Aoi! And I don't get to say that often!" Mimimi added. They were both clearly enjoying the unusual situation. But I was probably enjoying it more than anyone else.

"It's almost weird how happy I feel," I said.

"Tomozaki-kun? You'll pay for this!" the echoey voice scolded.

"I'm sorry—please have mercy on me," I said, attempting to mollify her so she wouldn't give me more assignments later.

"Tee-hee, you two sure are good friends," Kikuchi-san said.

"I know! It's amazing!" Izumi said.

"Oh n-no, not at all…," I said vaguely, trying in a mild panic to stop her from pursuing the topic.

"Hey, you guys, the ending's almost over!"

The music reached its grand finale with a *da-da-da-da!* There was a moment of silence. And then—

"Tree End!!"

"Oh my god, it's *The* End," I said, sharply correcting Takei as he once again misread the script. Come on—at least get the final line right!

HAVE YOU BEEN TURNED ON TO LIGHT NOVELS YET?

86—EIGHTY-SIX, VOL. 1–10

In truth, there is no such thing as a bloodless war. Beyond the fortified walls protecting the eighty-five Republic Sectors lies the "nonexistent" Eighty-Sixth Sector. The young men and women of this forsaken land are branded the Eighty-Six and, stripped of their humanity, pilot "unmanned" weapons into battle...

Manga adaptation available now!

WOLF & PARCHMENT, VOL. 1–6

The young man Col dreams of one day joining the holy clergy and departs on a journey from the bathhouse, Spice and Wolf. Winfiel Kingdom's prince has invited him to help correct the sins of the Church. But as his travels begin, Col discovers in his luggage a young girl with a wolf's ears and tail named Myuri who stowed away for the ride!

Manga adaptation available now!

SOLO LEVELING, VOL. 1–5

E-rank hunter Jinwoo Sung has no money, no talent, and no prospects to speak of—and apparently, no luck, either! When he enters a hidden double dungeon one fateful day, he's abandoned by his party and left to die at the hands of some of the most horrific monsters he's ever encountered.

Comic adaptation available now!